FLAME

THE FIREFIGHTERS OF DARLING BAY 3

RACHAEL HERRON

Cypress Hollow Yarns

Abigail's Shop

Lucy's Kiss

Naomi's Wish

Cora's Heart

Fiona's Flame

Eliza's Home

The Songbirds of Darling Bay

The Darling Songbirds

The Songbird's Call

The Songbird Sisters

The Firefighters of Darling Bay

Blaze

Burn

Flame

Heat

The Ballard Brothers of Darling Bay

On the Market

Build it Strong

Rock the Boat

Darling Bay Short Stories

A Darling Bay Christmas: Three Heartwarming Holiday Short Stories

Honeymooning: A Cypress Hollow Yarn Short Story

Women's Fiction Novels

The Ones Who Matter Most

Splinters of Light

Pack Up the Moon

Memoir

A Life in Stitches: Knitting My Way Through Love, Loss, and Laughter - Tenth Anniversary Edition

Unstuck: An Audacious Hunt for Home and Happiness

Nonfiction

Fast-Draft Your Memoir: Write Your Life Story in 45 Hours

Fast-Draft Your Memoir: The Workbook

Letters to New Authors: 29 Encouraging Letters to Your Inner Writer

Thrillers (as R. H. Herron)

Stolen Things

Hush Little Baby

CONTENTS

Chapter 1	1
Chapter 2	5
Chapter 3	10
Chapter 4	17
Chapter 5	27
Chapter 6	32
Chapter 7	41
Chapter 8	47
Chapter 9	52
Chapter 10	57
Chapter 11	61
Chapter 12	67
Chapter 13	74
Chapter 14	82
Chapter 15	90
Chapter 16	98
Chapter 17	104
Chapter 18	110
Chapter 19	116
Chapter 20	126
Chapter 21	129
Chapter 22	135
Chapter 23	141
Chapter 24	146
Chapter 25	153
Preview of Heat	158
HEAT - Chapter 1	159
Chapter 2	166
Chapter 3	173

Keep Reading! 183
About Rachael 185

Publisher's Note: This is a work of fiction. Names, characters, places, and incidents are a product of the author's imagination. Locales and public names are sometimes used for atmospheric purposes. Any resemblance to actual people, living or dead, or to businesses, companies, events, institutions, or locales is completely coincidental.

Flame / Rachael Herron. -- 2nd ed.

HGA Publishing

Paperback ISBN-13: 978-1-940785-26-4

CHAPTER 1

THE MAN CAME at her fast from the side, out of the shadows. His fist swung toward her jaw but Samantha ducked and caught the blow on her forearm. "No!" she yelled. "Stop!"

The man wheeled, coming back at her again. He roared, driving his fists against her shoulders, slamming her back into the brick wall, knocking the wind out of her.

Samantha took almost a full second to think, to dig inside herself for what she needed. The man was taller, broader, and outweighed her by sixty pounds. He had her pinned against the wall, and she could move nothing but her right leg.

That would be enough.

She kicked her foot left, driving her heel into her assailant's shin. His response was muffled but clearly displeased.

"No!" she managed to shout again. "No!" Her foot connected again, this time higher. She might have hit his kneecap.

One last time she yelled "Stop! Someone call 911!" The

man pulled back his head, as if her voice had hurt his ears. Samantha used the moment to shove her shoulder forward, freeing her right arm from his grip. Without a pause, she raised her fist and pummeled his ear, or where his ear would have been. She propped her foot against the wall and used it to push off from. The man lurched backward, struggling to keep his grip on her upper arms.

With a jerk of her neck, Samantha head-butted him, earning a muffled, "*Ooof.*"

Both her hands finally free, Samantha flew into motion. She jabbed, punched, kicked and clawed. She was a piston, each pump a blow. She didn't stop until the man was on the ground, curled onto his side, his arms protecting his head.

She'd done it. She'd won. Samantha's heart beat heavy and fast in her ears. No matter how many times it happened, she was always frightened. That was the point. Fighting past the fear. She turned to face the group behind her.

"This is when you run. Don't waste your breath calling for help at this point—right now you're using all your energy to put as much space between you and him. Get to a well-lit space or behind a locked door. Find a phone. Find a safe group of people and ask them to call 9 1 1. I call it *Down and Out.* He goes down, you get out."

A light laugh rippled around the room, but mostly Samantha heard rapid breathing as women took in quick sips of air. The first scene was always the second-worst part of the class. The worst part, of course, was the first fight each woman took part in.

The *best* part was the first scene each woman won, but they were still quite a way from learning how to do that.

"I know. This is intense. Take a deep breath."

The participants, to a woman, looked as if they might

fall right over, especially Linda McCracken, a woman who had been considering taking the class ever since her husband died a few months before, and was observing today. She'd looked nervous just walking in the door, but now she had a sheen of perspiration at her hairline and her hands were clenched at her sides.

Samantha said, "I mean *all* of you. Each one of you. You, too, Linda. Breathe. Right now. In…" A collective inhaled breath was followed by the out-breath. "Good."

Their eyes were all on Jim Hinds. Of course. Samantha had just beaten the tar out of him and he was still lying on the ground behind her.

"Jim's an old hand at this," she reassured them. "And he's trained for years to take this kind of beating. I've only been punching him for two months, but he worked down the coast for one of my trainers for a long time. He can take a lickin', for sure. Come on, Jim, stand up and strip out of the suit. Let them see who I was actually protecting myself from."

It was always a nice moment when Jim Hinds took off the padded gear and the women saw that the terrifying assailant, the stuff of nightmares, was actually the well-built librarian without his glasses on.

"Come on, Jim." Samantha turned. He was still lying exactly where he'd fallen. "Show them what you look like under all that padding."

But in the big white suit, Jim remained still.

There was another collected gasp. Linda McCracken started to weep.

"Jim?" Samantha leaned over him. "You all right, buddy?"

A strange wheeze was the only answer she got. Samantha dropped to her knees and pulled off Jim's helmet as gently as she could. His skin was pale and sweaty. His eyes met hers and telegraphed what he needed.

Samantha said clearly to Martina Miller, standing in the front row, "Use the pay phone by the front door. Call 911."

Martina's eyes widened. "Really?"

"This isn't part of the training. 911. *Now.*"

CHAPTER 2

HANK COULDN'T BELIEVE it.

Samantha Rowe. Again. How many times was he going to have to be thrown together with her? Not that he didn't want to be—no, wait. That was right. He *didn't* want to be.

Even Coin noticed it. "Doesn't it seem like you run into her everywhere you go, dude? What's it been, at least five times? You gonna ask her out or something?"

"No way." The truth was that he'd seen or talked to her *six* times since she'd gotten back to town. The first time had been when she'd had the car accident at the pier—he'd been so shocked to see her he'd dropped the jaws of life on his toe. Since then, he'd made up excuses to go call or text her, asking her silly questions like how long she was going to be in town, and what she thought of the acupuncture her sister practiced.

Thin excuses, all of them.

Then he'd heard she was seeing John Selzer, the used-car salesman who liked his women loud and accomplished in the flirting department, and Hank had realized that he'd fallen right back into his old pattern of crushing on Samantha Rowe, setting himself up for nothing but failure.

Yeah, he'd already spent years doing exactly that, before Samantha left town with a guy on a motorcycle, taking Hank's heart with her.

He wasn't doing *that* again.

But inside the community center, with her eyes on him, it had been all he could do not to pump Jim Hinds for information when they'd hooked him up to the 12-lead. Jim was awake by the time they got there, though his gray color made it clear he wasn't doing well. His rhythm had been far enough off that they'd packaged him for the ambulance, which had rumbled off code two, leaving Hank and Coin and Tox standing on the sidewalk in front of the center where Samantha Rowe was apparently teaching women to defend themselves.

"Yo! We're going to get pizza to take back to the station." Tox banged the engine door shut.

"No," started Hank. "I know what you're trying to—"

"Back soon," said Coin with a grin.

"You both suck," Hank growled. "Hurry it up."

Because Tox and Coin were both going in to Junior's Pizzeria, Hank was the one who, by default, had drawn the short straw and had to stay behind with the engine.

Normally it didn't bother him. He was, after all, the most junior of the crew, and it happened to him a couple of times a week. He got to put the radio on the channel he liked (country, which had the added benefit of seriously irritating Tox when he got back in the rig). He didn't mind talking to citizens as they walked by—and everyone had something to say when they passed a fire engine—even when they were actively criticizing the department. *I can't believe you're just sitting here, waiting for someone to have a fire. Hard day, son? Are my tax dollars paying you to look at your phone?*

Hank would just shrug and say, "Someone's gotta do it, sir." Because those same citizens were the ones who would expect them to arrive at their homes twenty seconds after they dialed 911, and on those days, they were nothing but grateful to see the fire engine turning down their street. Some of the guys hated taking the flak, but Hank didn't mind. His shoulders were broad enough.

But right now? Sitting in front of Samantha Rowe's self-defense class while his partners got pizza? Tox and Coin were jerks, plain and simple. It never paid to admit a weakness to anyone in the fire department, never.

And Samantha was a weakness, all right.

That moment, what was it, eight months or so ago now? When they'd pulled up in the engine, when they'd seen that car perched on the edge of the pier, smashed halfway through the railing, teetering and swaying—Hank had known that whoever was inside had to get out, and fast. If the car hit the water, it would be bad. Really bad.

But then Hank had gotten to the side window and looked inside the vehicle to see Samantha Rowe in the passenger seat—completely unconscious.

The girl who had broken his heart. The woman he'd compared all other girlfriends to—it hadn't been fair to them, of course. He knew that. But he couldn't help it. When he was dating Joanne, he'd compared her plain brown eyes to Samantha's brilliant green ones. When he and Nicole had been an item, he'd remembered Samantha's enormous, almost startling laugh, placing it next to Nicole's timid one.

He'd learned about Platonic ideals in a college class (had she been in that class too? No, probably not. If she had been, he wouldn't remember a darn thing about the subject). Samantha was his Platonic ideal of the perfect woman—confident, beautiful, smart, and funny.

And there, on that pier, she'd been an inch away from death, and he was one of the men working to save her.

In a movie, he would have been the one to cut open the door, to pull her to safety just before the car plunged to the water so far below.

In reality, he was one of a team of guys who worked fast and accurately. Tox pulled her out and Coin was the one who helped the medics lift her onto the backboard.

In a movie, her lashes would have fluttered just as she was being wheeled away. They would have locked eyes and exchanged pieces of their souls as she was loaded into the ambulance.

In reality, she didn't wake up for hours. Not until she was at the hospital, and when he went to check on her, he'd been rewarded by a super-friendly greeting. The kind one gave an old acquaintance from college, in fact. Which was exactly what he was to her. They should catch up! Have coffee sometime!

Damn it. He'd pretty much planned on never seeing her again, and now that she was in town, and he knew he was going to have to, he'd planned on just trying to stay away from her.

Instead? He'd stepped right into the friend zone. She'd grabbed him one morning at Mabel's Cafe and bought him a cruller. Bought *him* a cruller. Wouldn't even let him buy her a coffee.

If he could just get her out of his system, once, for good...

What would that be like?

How would it feel to go on a date with a nice woman he

didn't compare to Samantha? Maybe he could finally make a go of it with someone, someone he could introduce to his Gramma Maureen, the woman who'd raised him. Someone he could settle down and fall in love with, someone he could have those babies everyone else was having. Hank dreamed of kids, a passel of them, running around the house, filling it with noise and dirt and rambunctiousness.

He'd just never been able to picture anyone to have them with. Anyone that didn't look like Samantha, that was. Every girl of his dreams that he imagined had that same thick brown hair hanging to her mid-back, each one had those sparkling green eyes and that nose that slanted upward, right at the very tip. Every dream girl had her figure, too: just right, not too slim, with—let's face it—a rack that just wouldn't quit.

Three women exited the Darling Bay Community Center chattering excitedly about the drama of Jim Hinds hitting the dirt. One smiled up at him, and he smiled back, his teeth clenched. Hopefully Samantha had a lot to do inside and wouldn't come out till they'd left. She probably needed to put whatever they worked with away, and probably had to close windows and doors and set the alarm...

No such luck.

Samantha waved at him cheerfully as she came out of the building.

"Hank! I'm so glad you were on the engine that came to help Jim!" She stood at the foot of the open door and looked up at him. "Where are the other guys? Can I come up?" She started climbing the steps before he answered, leaving him to scramble backward in surprise.

"Whoa," was the only thing he could think of to say.

CHAPTER 3

"WHAT?" SHE PULLED back. The way Samantha barreled forward, Hank knew she was probably used to having to self-correct. "I'm not supposed to be up here?

Not technically, no. She wasn't. The only people allowed on board were either paid by the Darling Bay Fire Department or specially cleared for ride-alongs. If Chief Barger rolled by and looked up to see a citizen in one of his rigs? Heads would roll, and the first head spinning would be Hank's.

But instead of telling Samantha Rowe that she couldn't climb up, Hank reached a hand down to help pull her up. He felt that stupid grin cross his face, the one he always got when she was anywhere around. *Dummy.* "Come on. Watch your head there." He pointed her to the spare jumpseat. "Are you okay?"

"That was terrible! So scary!" she said, leaning forward so she could rest her elbows on her knees. For a moment, he forgot she was talking about Jim Hinds and thought she was talking about the climb up. She'd always done that to him—

confused him until he didn't know what was up or down. Her hair, that wonderful brown waterfall, fell forward and, for a moment, hid her eyes. Was she crying? Hank felt two simultaneous urges: to leap forward and wrap his arms around her and to throw himself out of the rig. No *way* was he worrying about her again. No way.

Samantha looked up at him, but instead of tears, her bright green eyes were sparkling with excitement. "That was *amazing*, what you did."

They really hadn't done much. They'd assessed Jim and strapped him to a gurney. His pulse on the 12-lead was strong enough that they didn't even go code three. "Nah."

She laughed, that sound as pretty and sweet as whatever light scent she was wearing, the scent that Coin with his dog's nose would be able to pick up as soon as he climbed back on board. "You saved a man's life."

Saving lives was what they did. And Jim hadn't been a save so much as a push to the hospital where he definitely needed to be seen. Something was wrong with the guy, but nothing immediate. "He'll be fine. He'll be home tonight, nursing those bruises that got put on him by your group of aggressive women. What were you doing to him in there?"

Samantha flapped her hand. "Ah, you know. Beatin' the tar out of him. Every girl's gotta learn how sometime."

"It looked like you were killing him."

"No, it didn't! Did you see how well he was suited up?"

"It wasn't easy to get through all that padding to get the leads on, so yeah. But did you see that bruise on his right arm?"

Samantha looked a little guilty. "It's possible that Myra Tenbottom got a little carried away with her kicking. But that just means she was *really* into it."

Hank straightened his legs. The hardest thing about

being the firefighter in the back of the rig was that it wasn't big enough to fully stretch out. Right now while the door was still open was the ideal time to do it. "So, what is it that you do in there, anyway?"

"I teach women how to defend themselves against would-be attackers."

"That's great."

Samantha looked surprised. "Really?"

"Of course."

"The reaction I've gotten in this town doesn't always go that way."

Darling Bay could be a little provincial, but... "What do you mean?"

Samantha looked out the small window as if looking for someone. "Men usually wonder out loud who it is we're going to beat up." She made air quotes around the last two words. "I always tell them that if they're that worried about it, maybe they shouldn't be around the women that train at Daring Darling."

Hank nodded. It was a good answer. "I like it. What about women?"

"I get one of two responses. Either they say how cool it sounds and how much they want their niece, sister, mother, and aunt to take it, or I get silence."

He filled in the blank in his mind. "That's what you don't want to get."

"Yeah. That means it's too late, and they should have already known what to do in the past."

"In Darling Bay?"

"Everywhere. In every town. One in five women will survive rape or attempted rape, and ninety-seven percent of rapists won't ever stay a night in jail."

"Well, heck." Hank stretched out his hands, looking at the knuckles. "I hate that so much I can't even stand it."

"Well, yeah."

"What can I do to help?"

"What?" She sounded startled.

"People have to ask you that."

"Strangely enough, no."

"How long have you been doing it?" Hank had been seeing the flyers up around town for at least the last four months—Daring Darling Defense, a silhouette of a woman standing proudly upright in front of a darkened door.

"Seventeen weeks." Samantha sounded proud. "But it's going really well."

"Until you knocked out your attacker."

Samantha barked a short laugh. "Yeah. *Crap*. He'll be back. Right?" Her eyes were worried. "Right?"

"Maybe?" Hank hated to lie, even when he should.

"But you don't think so?"

"A guy with that coloring?"

"You mean pink and white?"

"He left out of here gray. That's not a good sign for either his heart or his lungs. He might be out a while."

Samantha pulled up her legs and wrapped her arms around them. "No. I need him."

"He's your only guy?"

"I have another one, Wally, but he's so skinny that the women just toss him around like a teacup."

"Wally Atkins? Isn't he over sixty?"

She looked chagrined. "Well, it's pretty easy for the more advanced to block him."

"Block him? They'll kill him."

"I know." She sighed, blowing a breath out. A brown curl swung next to her face and Hank tried not to notice how her chest rose in her T-shirt with each breath. That rack of hers had only gotten better with time. "I need to come up with a better plan."

"I'll do it." Hank knew as soon as he said it that he wanted it. He wanted to help. To save her. Okay, to save her business. But wasn't that kind of similar? Even while his inner voice told him he was just falling into the same old pattern, he said, "I'll help. If you want me to."

"You'd train to be an attacker?"

"Yeah."

"Do you have any idea what that entails?"

"Beyond being beaten up by a bunch of angry women? No."

"First of all," she raised one finger, "you'll have to realize that it's not a bunch of angry women. It's a bunch of women appropriating their much-deserved autonomy, realizing that they don't have to rely on a man to take care of them. It's a bunch of women figuring out they're as strong as or stronger than many men, and that they can learn how to use their bodies to their fullest potential in terms of protection."

"That sounds a lot better."

"And two, you'll have to learn how to wear the suit and come at a woman." She made a stabbing motion at the bridge of her nose as if she was pushing invisible glasses back up.

"I can do that."

"Can you?"

Hank rubbed his face. He wanted to. He shouldn't want to. He should just stay out of Samantha Rowe's way. For his own sake. "Yes."

"What if I came at you right now?"

"Huh?"

"What if I tried to hit you? Would you even be able to fend me off, let alone push me to the floor or against a wall?"

The unbidden image of him pushing her against the door of the engine, his lips on hers, filled his mind.

Samantha came off her seat and launched herself at him, her arm swinging. She stopped just before her fist made contact with his cheek. Hank scrambled sideways and almost fell out of the open door of the rig. Holding on with one hand, his foot twisted on the outer step, he took a quick look around to see if anyone had seen his more-than-ungraceful lurch from the seat.

"No," said Samantha, folding herself back onto her seat.

"No, what?" Hank pretended he'd been making a move to check the radio in the front. He turned it off and back on, waiting for the power-up beeping to stop before he said, "Was that a test?"

"You failed."

"What? Because of my lightning-fast reflexes?"

"Because you didn't come at me."

"Hey, now."

"You have to be able to come at a woman. With no holds barred. You can't be afraid to hurt her."

"Um. I *would* be afraid to hurt her. I'm bigger and stronger than ninety percent of the women I saw coming out of the studio, and Greta Wagner doesn't count—she's a professional bodybuilder."

Samantha looked startled. "I *knew* she was stronger than she was letting on. But that's not what I'm talking about. What you're training them to do is to feel a man's strength, the force of someone coming at them with all their might, and then getting it done anyway. Fighting back. And winning."

"What if they don't win? How do you keep them safe so that your attacker doesn't hurt them?"

She shot him a quick, amused look. "Oh, yeah. You're going to be fun to train. Are you sure about this? You think you can handle it?"

Handle being around Samantha Rowe? For hours and hours? No way could he handle it. He didn't *want* to handle it. But he found himself nodding anyway. And if he got to help one woman feel safer as a result, he could call that a well-spent day.

"Good," she said. "Are you off-duty tomorrow?"

He nodded again, dumbly.

"Come by the center at nine?"

Hank said, "I'll be there."

Boy howdy, would he ever. And damn it, just like that, the fire was back in him when he thought of Samantha Rowe. The years he'd spent getting over her were gone up in a puff of smoke that smelled like flowery shampoo.

He didn't even want those years back. When it came right down to it, he didn't mind as much as he should. When Tox and Coin climbed back onboard, Coin flinging two pizzas onto the spare seat so recently vacated by Samantha Rowe's delicious backside, he didn't even care that they'd bought pepperoni again, instead of the sausage he preferred.

It was all good.

He was going to see Samantha Rowe tomorrow. And maybe, just maybe, get to tackle the heck out of her and not get in trouble for it.

CHAPTER 4

S AMANTHA BROUGHT INSIDE the bag of lemons she'd just picked from her sister Grace's back-yard tree.

"I got twenty. And man, do some of them look funny. You have some lemons out there that have screaming little sour faces, did you know that? Is that because it's winter or something?"

Her sister smiled at her. "I forgot to rein you in. Sorry. I was just going to make a little lemonade. Five would have done."

"Hand me the squeezer-thingie. We'll just make a crap-ton."

"Is that the technical measurement?"

"Yep," said Samantha. "I know this from when I worked on the swamp boat in Louisiana."

Grace bumped her hip, moving her from in front of the oven where an apple-cinnamon pie was about to come out. "I don't get what a boat in a swamp has to do with lemons."

Samantha plunked all the lemons from the bag into the sink and began to rinse them. "We were famous for it. Alligator sightings and the best spiked lemonade in the bayou." She fell silent as she remembered the smell of the swamp, the green earthiness of it, rising from all around, the sharp scent of the lemons cutting through it, and the fogginess in her head when she woke up every morning in the little hanging bunk she and two other waitresses shared on the riverboat. The almost constant morning hangover, only alleviated by liberal application of the spiked lemonade the boat tour was so famous for.

She'd lost months on that boat. Nothing to show for them but a higher tolerance for vodka, and her tolerance had already been too high.

Grace said, "Well, I guess you can use the lemonade skills for the rest of your life, anyway." Her voice was kind, and Samantha appreciated it. Her sister had been pretty judgmental when she'd first come back around, and why wouldn't she be? Samantha had been a wreck for ten years of her life, for every year she spent in her twenties. When she'd finally gotten clean and sober, it had taken a while for Samantha to believe it of herself, let alone for anyone else to. Now it wasn't so much a *hard* thing as it was a thing. Her thing. She didn't drink today. That's what she knew. Hopefully she wouldn't drink tomorrow, either. But she didn't think about it.

She thought about today and the sugary tartness of the lemonade she was making. As she sliced the first of them, she could feel her mouth start to pucker.

It felt good, being here. With her sister.

"Is Tox stopping by?"

Grace shook her head and sliced the pie. "No. He's working."

"Oh, of course. I knew that. I saw him earlier, actually."

Grace looked up. "Really? Where?"

"At the community center."

"What happened?"

"Jim Hinds fainted during a class."

"Is he okay?"

"Should be fine." Samantha had gone by to see Jim after talking to Hank. At the hospital, Jim had seemed shaken and pale, but in good spirits. Not in similar spirits was his wife, who'd been furious. Jim had told Samantha he would be out for a couple of months while he figured out what was wrong with him, but Allie Hinds had followed her into the hall and had told her that her husband wouldn't be attacking any more women for Samantha.

It was too bad. Jim not only hit hard, he laughed hard, too. Her students felt safe with him. Sure, he was terrifying the first time he came at them for real, but then, when they stood their ground, and he had to fall down or back off or run, he was the first to congratulate them when he took off his helmet.

"He's not going to be able to come back."

"Oh, that's no good. Hey, be careful with that knife, would you?"

Samantha held it up. "Lady, I know how to fight off men armed with machetes. You think I'm scared of a little kitchen knife like this?" She set the next lemon on the cutting board and promptly sliced through the tip of her finger.

"Ow." The blood came fast as Samantha held it up to look at the damage. "Double ow. Maybe triple."

Grace laughed.

"I can't believe you're *laughing* at me right now," Samantha said as she wound a paper towel around her finger. "I'm probably dying."

Grace straightened her face, and Samantha could tell it wasn't easy. "Do you think you need stitches?"

Samantha peeked under the towel. "Not more than one or two."

The grin on Grace's face fell. "Really truly?"

"No. I'm probably fine. It'll stop bleeding in a second." She paused. "Or I'll *bleed to death* because my sister *doesn't care*."

Grace, looking reassured, shrugged. "I warned you about that knife. Tox has been sharpening them every time he comes over."

"Why doesn't he just move in? Now that you've got your child, and by that I mean me, out of the house?" Samantha had recently rented an apartment over the bagel shop. The fact that she got a discount on rent for working the register a couple of mornings a week had sealed the already-sweet deal of the bay-facing one bedroom.

Grace placed a piece of pie on a paper plate and carefully covered it with saran wrap. Samantha knew she probably didn't realize that she was as transparent as the plastic —that piece of pie would be Samantha's piece to take home with her. The rest of the pie would go to the fire station. If Samantha didn't like the big, loud Tox as much as she did, she'd probably be sickened by it.

Instead, she found herself wondering what it must be like to have that kind of relationship with someone.

And most disconcertingly, she found herself wondering about Hank.

Grace slipped in front of her, making short work of slicing the lemons and using the hand-press to get the most liquid out. "Just sit. Keep me company."

"What's the lemonade for, anyway? You've never been that into lemonade."

Grace colored prettily and Samantha groaned. "You're taking that to him, too? Martha Stewart, huh? I think you need to add a vanilla bean and a spring of wild rosemary to that, don't forget."

"You were *just* trying to pair us off into the same living arrangement."

"That's different. I want him to live with you and for him to mow your lawn for you."

Dreamily, Grace said, "Oh, he mows my lawn, all right..."

Samantha held up her hands. "Enough. That's way more than I needed to know, anyway. Hey, what if I asked Hank Coffee to help out at Darling Defense?"

Grace blinked. "Really?"

"To be my attacker when Wally can't be there," she clarified.

Grace shook her head. "Are you sure about that? Do you want me to tell you what I really think?"

"I want your opinion. Of what you think he would be like to work with. That's all." Samantha took a deep breath. She loved her sister with all her heart, and sometimes she just wished that for *once*, Grace could not try to manage things."

She watched Grace take a matching breath as she put down the knife. "Tox adores him. Wait. Let me correct that. Tox doesn't adore anyone—"

"Except you."

"—okay, but he really trusts Hank. He says he's a good listener."

"I remember that about him."

Grace slapped the top of the counter. "Right, right, I forgot for a minute. You freaking *dated* him, when, in junior college?"

Samantha nodded. "Way back when we were too stupid to figure anything out except how to drop any class that started before noon."

"And that's why he was all moony after your accident. That's right. Why are you asking me, then? You know him way better than I ever could. I, for example, never slept with him."

Samantha opened her mouth and then closed it. She hadn't slept with Hank back then. For some reason, that made the memory of him more...special. It felt stupid, and she wouldn't admit it to her sister, but Hank had been better than just some guy she'd randomly hooked up with while drunk at a frat party. She'd really *liked* Hank, with his lanky limbs and shy brown eyes and that mop of scruffy surfer-boy hair, dark with blond highlights colored by the sun.

And then Vicente had come along, bragging on his arrest record—who else but a rebellious teenager grown into a looking-for-excitement woman would fall for that?—and roaring out on his Harley. Young Samantha, idiotic Samantha, had dumped Hank almost unceremoniously. She'd taken him out, yeah. To a little bar in town, the Wooden Duck, if she remembered right. She'd bought him a beer and had told him that there was someone else. He'd looked upset. She hadn't had enough alcohol yet that night to wipe that out of her mind.

Then Vicente had pushed through the bar doors—because, again, the idiotic Samantha had thought she could get everything done in one place, break up with one guy, meet up with another. She'd left with Vicente that night, wrapping one arm around his waist, waving with the other hand back at Hank.

How would her life have been different if she'd jumped

off Vicente's motorcycle while it was still in the lot, if she'd raced back to be with Hank, instead?

But no. Samantha leaped before she looked. She decided to do things before weighing the consequences. Sometimes that turned out great. Once she'd ended up waitressing for six months at a surfer bar in Molokai, sand between her toes.

And once, she'd ended up in rehab after an overdose.

They say it took some people a long time to hit rock bottom. Samantha knew she'd been lucky. Her bottom had been no place to stay, no job, nowhere to go, her sister finally refusing her calls. She'd come close to dying herself that time, and she didn't want that ever to happen again.

So yeah, jumping off that motorcycle would have earned her some road rash, but might have saved a lot of heartache over the years.

"He offered to help with the classes. After the ambulance took Jim away."

"What did you say?"

"What could I say? I think he'd be perfect, if he can learn to hit a girl."

Grace shuddered. "I hate it when you say that."

"People hit girls," said Samantha. "It's better if women know how to hit back if necessary."

"Remember when you were tutoring kids? You helped them write their college essays. Wasn't that a nicer job? More easy on the...hands? And body? I hate that you're taking punches." Grace measured the sugar, and Samantha knew she wouldn't ever go over or under the recommended amount, whereas Samantha liked to pour in as much extra sugar as she could, until the liquid wouldn't take any more. She'd learned it from their mother, who loved sweet things, just like Samantha. Their mother had died of cancer before she'd been able to do all the things she'd wanted to, and Samantha had recovered slower than the aptly-named Grace, so much more like their prosaic, sensible father.

Samantha pulled the paper towel more tightly around her finger. "We do the same job, if you think about it."

"Huh. Acupuncture as self-defense? Or are you looking at it the other way around?"

"You punch people with needles to be more healthy. I needle people until they throw punches in order to be more safe." Samantha felt pleased with her turn of phrase, awkward though it was.

"That might be a bit over-the-top. How about we're both helping people to be better humans?"

"Okay, Rainshadow Warrior, put your incense and moon crystals down before someone gets hurt." Samantha pulled off a piece of the pie crust and popped it in her mouth.

Grace hit her lightly on the knee. "He's cute, you know."

Samantha frowned. "Do you think so?" She tried to play dumb but knew it would never fly.

"Come on. And I know you do, too."

It was a good point. Samantha *did* think Hank was cute. He'd grown into those long limbs—no longer lanky, he'd filled out with what seemed like all muscle. He was gorgeous, in fact, still with that mop of floppy brown surfer hair, those big dark eyes, those chiseled cheek bones, and his chest so wide it looked like he did push-ups all day. "You might be right. I don't think I should give him the job."

Grace closed her eyes. "So you're going to change your mind again."

Samantha gritted her teeth. She hated it when Grace said that. Just because Samantha frequently thought about things and decided on new courses of action didn't mean that she was as fickle as her sister thought. "It might be weird. With our history and all."

Grace said, "Hmm."

"And then there's the whole thing that he's Tox's partner..."

"One of his coworkers."

"They ride in the same fire engine. Every day."

Grace shook her head. "Not every day. They get days off. I don't understand why you're changing your mind on this. Give the guy a chance. Look, come with me to the fire station tonight when I go to visit Tox. Bring the lemonade. The guys'll love it."

"No way." Samantha grabbed her coat—too thin for the cold weather outside—and checked her jeans pocket for her keys. "Hey, do me a favor, would you?"

"No, no, *no*." Grace held up her hands. "I'm not telling him you're backing out."

"Please?" Samantha clapped her hands together, prayer-like. "Pretty please? For me?"

"I'm a founding member of your business, right?"

"The only one I have."

"So this member says no. I'm not telling him. *You* tell him you changed your mind."

"Gracie. I can't. I don't want to hurt him."

"What, you think he hasn't recovered from when you broke up with him a million years ago?"

Samantha didn't say anything and just kept her eyes on Grace's. If there was any chance that Hank still minded her leaving him in that bar so many years ago, it wasn't fair to hurt him again.

"Gah. Fine. What am I supposed to tell him?"

"That Jim got better."

"No."

"That I found someone else."

"Who?"

"It doesn't matter." Hank, of *all* people, couldn't be the attacker for Darling Defense. Why hadn't she thought it through? Hank would probably sign his girlfriend up for the class—because a guy like him *had* to have a beautiful little girlfriend—and then Samantha would have to be friends with her. And that quickly became one of the worst ideas Samantha had ever thought of. "Anyone. You. Tox. I don't care."

Grace sighed heavily. "Fine," her sister said. "Whatever. I'll clean up the mess. Again."

Samantha hated with all her heart that that was exactly what Grace was doing. But she couldn't hurt Hank again, not even one tiny little mosquito's worth of hurt, and heck. She was used to her sister being disappointed in her.

CHAPTER 5

HANK HAD NEVER noticed the apartment over the bagel shop, even though he stopped for coffee there at least once a week. The staircase that led up from the back parking lot was rickety, the handhold loose. The small back porch trembled as he stood on it, and he noticed that there wasn't even a bulb screwed in to the porch fixture.

He knocked on the glass panel in the door. *Calm down.* He was being ridiculous, but the nervousness he'd woken up with hadn't gone away—in fact, he'd had to leave his coffee half-drunk on the counter at home.

Jeez. He wasn't picking her up for a date, after all. This was a business thing. All business.

Sure, all business, but he'd dreamed of her mouth last night. The way her body had felt against his—that wasn't business at all. That had just been so hot it had hurt to roll over.

The fact that she hadn't opened the door yet, though, was weird.

He knocked again, and the glass panes clattered in the

door. They were loose enough he bet he could slip one pane out without even breaking it. If there was one thing he and his firefighter brethren were good at, it was breaking into people's homes. Most older people left their doors unlocked in case they needed help, and Darling Bay was safe enough for it to be okay most of the time. But younger residents still fell in their bathrooms or had sudden asthma attacks. Medical problems often rendered healthy people unable to unlock a door in a timely fashion. And when every second counted, firefighters broke down doors, bashed in windows, tore off locked screens, and lifted sliding glass doors off their rails.

Curiosity got the better of him. Hank fit the flat of his palm to the pane and jiggling it lightly, used an upward pressure. Sure enough, the glass lifted enough in its small frame that he was able to get his thumb under it. He slid it out, toward him. Great. Now he'd have to make sure it was fixed before he left, but it should be easy enough to slip it back in.

Samantha wasn't safe, after all. He'd just proved that. Anyone could do this, any two-bit burglar with a small slice of imagination. The real question remained: could he reach down to unlock the door?

Hank peeked in the now open hole, and still seeing no motion, convinced himself that by now, it was really his moral duty to check on her. She was expecting him—she should have answered the door by now.

He put his arm in and down, reaching toward the latch.

His hand was slapped so hard he shouted. *"Holy crap! It's Hank!"* He jerked his hand back out and almost dropped the pane.

The door was yanked open. On the other side, Samantha was wrapped in nothing but black plastic-framed glasses and a thin pink towel. The towel looked fantastic, actually. Samantha would probably look good in PPEs, but in a short piece of fabric, still dripping, she looked beyond amazing.

She also looked good when she was mad. That was a new revelation, but not a surprising one.

"*What?*"

"I just said it was me. Sorry. I like your glasses." Hank rubbed the back of his hand. "What did you hit me with?"

She brandished her weapon.

"Fly swatter. Nicely played." Hank wondered for a moment what would have happened if he *had* gained access to her apartment and Samantha was just fine? How much damage could she have done to him? The thought was sobering, and while kind of hot, not something he wanted to find out.

"I'm sorry." He held up the piece of rounded glass. "But this was loose. Anyone could get in."

"I forget my keys in the house sometimes. I *like* it like that. What are you doing here?"

Honest confusion filled Hank. Had he gotten the date wrong? No, she'd clearly said the words *tomorrow* and *my apartment*. "I thought we said..."

Samantha grimaced. "Grace."

"What about her?"

"Did she come by the station last night?"

Even more confused now that this was something about her sister, Hank said, "I think she did? We were out on a call, but there was pie on the counter when we got back and Tox said it was his favorite."

"Oh, man."

"What's wrong? Are you okay?" She looked okay. Good grief, she looked so damn okay...

"I have to put on some clothes."

No, you don't, darlin'. The words were almost spoken before he shut his mouth again. Something about Samantha Rowe scrambled Hank's brain like eggs in hot butter. "Sure, sure." Hank was pretty certain his initial response showed on his face, though. He didn't actually mind that much.

Samantha spun on her heel, heading for the far door in the small room. She shut it quietly behind her.

So this had something to do with Grace? And a pie?

Hank took the opportunity of Samantha being gone to explore her apartment. The whole thing was as small as the kitchen at Station One, but it was warm. Welcoming, even though it was probably less than five hundred square feet, with only room for a bed and a tiny sofa. The kitchen sink had to be against code since it was an arm's reach from the bathroom. The whole place looked like it needed be upgraded, actually. The light over the sink blinked and the old Formica on the countertop was stained with age. But she had color everywhere, from her violet bedspread to the grass green pillows topping the tiny blue couch. Cobalt glasses rested next to yellow plates. The overall result was a happy jumble.

French doors gave light on the west wall, even covered with a thin piece of purple fabric. He pushed aside the curtain, and let himself onto the porch. That door was also unlocked.

But what a reason to leave a door open. If he had French doors that opened onto a view of Darling Bay in all its frank beauty, Hank would want to be able to push them open at a second's notice, too.

He leaned on the railing, sucking the cold morning ocean air deeply into his lungs. Man, even growing up here, even looking at the marina every day, it just never got old.

Today it felt like he was seeing the docks for the first time, and indeed, he supposed that he'd never seen the boats from quite this angle. Sure, he'd seen them from the street hundreds of times, and from the top of the bank building where the fire department launched the 4th of July fireworks, but never from here, just one story up. In the harbor, at least thirty boats bobbed, their masts making the clanking, jingling noise Hank associated with home. The air smelled of yeast from downstairs and of cold metal.

Below, on the sidewalk, Tonia Pringle caught sight of him and did a double take, almost losing hold of the leash she had on her tiny chihuahua, Mr. Chester. Awesome. Now gossip would fly. Tonia was best friends with Mrs. Finch, and within an hour, most of Darling Bay would know that Hank had been spotted on Samantha Rowe's balcony.

Interesting to notice how little he minded.

He gave a short wave to Tonia. "Good morning! How's Mr. Chester doing today?"

Tonia scooped up her dog and scurried off without saying anything. The Homeless Petes—both of them—were sharing a bottle on the bus stop bench and laughed as Tonia hustled.

So did Hank.

A sunbeam broke through the fog and bounced across the small balcony, lighting the old painted wood a brighter blue. The light matched his mood. It was going to be a terrific day.

If Samantha decided she wanted him there, that was.

CHAPTER 6

I N THE BATHROOM, Samantha shot another glance at her cell phone. Nothing back from Grace yet. Grace, who usually texted back within a minute. She sent another one. *Were you going to TELL me, at least? I was NAKED when he came.*

Nothing.

Fine.

She could do this herself. She was a business owner, after all, albeit a new one. Prior to this, the only business she'd ever been in charge of was her paper route at age eleven which she'd lost when she decided she didn't like getting up in the dark before school. Since then, she'd always worked *for* someone. She'd done a million different jobs, most of them legal, but someone else had always paid her.

But now she was her own boss, and women like her had to do the hard things as well as the awesomely fun things.

Like firing someone.

Well.

Was it actually firing if they'd never really been hired? It's not like she and Hank had discussed a wage, or times of work. He hadn't even proved he could do the job yet.

Samantha jerked a comb through her wet hair. *Shoot.* If she'd *known* he was coming, that Grace hadn't done her dirty work for her—okay, she did feel guilty for asking her to —she would have had time to figure out what to wear, to pick a shade of lipstick that looked good. Instead, the Samantha he was going to see was her regular old morning self, the one with no mascara and no contacts. Her glasses! She touched the rim of them with her fingers. She was almost legally blind without them, but she hadn't worn them in public for years.

But he was just going to have to deal with her as she was.

She blinked in the mirror.

Silly. It was silly to feel this upset. Her nerves twanged as if someone were striking them with a hammer.

She put on jeans from the tiny bathroom closet—the only closet the minuscule apartment had. She grabbed a clean black T-shirt, and not her lowest-cut one, either. She could be professional. Hide the double-Ds a little bit. She gathered back her hair into a ponytail and pushed her glasses more firmly onto her nose.

Great. Now she looked just about as stern as a person could be and not be shushing someone at a library for laughing.

Hank wasn't in the living room, and she could tell with one quick glance that he couldn't be hiding in her bedroom, which was so small she'd gotten the apartment at a studio rate.

The doors were open to the balcony and the scent of

salt and fresh bagels blew through. Of course he was in her favorite spot.

There he was, sitting on one of her two iron chairs, a beam of sunshine resting across his knees like it was curling up in his lap.

"Howdy," he said, his voice honeyed and slow.

Samantha felt her knees quake in a way she hadn't expected. "Good morning." She sat. "Cold out here."

"You have more clothes on now," he pointed out. Unnecessarily.

"I do."

"Your glasses are cute on you. I never pictured you wearing them."

"Thanks. I hate them."

"They're hot. *Damn* it."

Samantha jumped. "What?"

"I'm really trying not to flirt with you."

The abrupt confession startled her. "Okay. Why?" *Why was she asking?* She didn't want to know the answer.

Except that she did. Very much so.

"Because you're going to be my boss. Ish."

"Ish," she repeated weakly.

He leaned back in the chair and looked good doing it. Did he have any idea what he looked like out here in the sun on her porch? In his dark-washed jeans and red flannel worn open over a blue T-shirt, the only thing he was missing was a cowboy hat.

It was good he wasn't wearing one. Good grief. She would *not* be able to handle that with any kind of equanimity. Not like she had any, anyway.

"Yeah. I mean, the fire department is my first love. Obviously. But I can handle a second job, too. Lots of guys in the department do."

Samantha felt a small smile creep across her face. "Remember how crazy you were in college about getting that job?" She remembered more now, looking at him. She remembered the way he'd told her his dearest dream, to save someone's life while wearing the badge of the Darling Bay Fire Department. He'd been going to school for his fire science degree, and he'd already put himself through paramedic training. He'd been only twenty-one then. So young.

"How long did it actually take you to get hired?"

"I got in on the first try." He grinned, and Samantha noticed how straight and white his teeth were.

"How old were you when you did?" She'd left with Vicente not long after he'd held her on the beach, his arms wrapped tightly around her as they looked up at the moon and whispered their dreams to each other.

"Twenty-two."

They were both thirty-three now. "Such a long time ago."

"Feels like just about a minute to me. Oh, hey, big fella." Hank stretched out his fingers to the huge orange cat that had just jumped from her neighbor's balcony railing to hers.

"That's Anchor. He lives with my neighbor Gus. I'm not sure who's more interesting, Gus, or the cat."

Anchor wound its body around Hank's legs and then leaped—nimbly for a cat who must have weighed twenty pounds—into the puddle of sunshine in Hank's lap.

"He likes me," said Hank, scratching the cat behind the ears.

She blurted it out, unable to keep it in a moment longer. "I can't hire you."

He blinked. Those long lashes of his. She'd forgotten about those.

"You're firing me?"

"No," she groaned. "I just can't hire you."

"Why not?"

"Because."

"That's a terrible reason, you know."

"I know."

"You're really bad at this."

She shoved her glasses higher onto her nose. "We have history."

"We do. And you just pointed out the fact that it's ancient."

It was. "But it's there."

"History's a good thing for friends to have."

Samantha could hear the cat purring from where she sat. Traitor. Anchor usually loved her. "But we're not friends." She wanted to yank back the words the second they left her mouth. They sounded cruel. Hurtful. And she'd meant to be the absolute opposite. "I'm sorry. What I mean is that—"

Hank interrupted her smoothly. "You meant that friends call each other on their birthdays and grab a quick bite together when they're in the neighborhood."

"Yeah!" That was, actually, what she meant. They'd never done that. She hadn't been around.

"And they know when one of them is freaking out for no apparent reason."

"Wait a minute."

He leaned forward. Behind him, to the northwest, a cluster of high-school kids—their only nod to the winter cold their hooded sweatshirts—jockeyed for position on the low stone wall that separated the first pier from the board-walk. "To the scientifically trained eye—which mine is, by the way—you're freaking out for no apparent reason."

"I have a very good reason."

"And that is…"

What was it again? This close to him, his malted-milk-colored eyes dancing in the cold sun, so close she could smell the clean fragrance of soap and maybe shaving cream, Samantha was having a hard time remembering what that reason was. "Because it wouldn't be fair. To anyone. I'm scared…" She stopped. She wasn't *scared*. Samantha didn't get scared. "I mean, I would worry that…"

"That you would hurt me again?"

"Maybe?"

"Don't worry, sugar. You can't."

"Good." She meant it. "You're happy, then?"

One of the teen girls on the wall gave a loud laugh followed by a sharp scream.

"What the hell?" Hank twisted in his chair. Anchor leaped off his lap with a complaint.

And before Samantha could even figure out what was going on below, Hank was over the railing, literally. He leaped over her rail, turning in midair as he grasped the edge of a wooden beam. Before she could even lean all the way over the rail, he'd used the drainpipe to steady him as he took the last long leap to the ground. Looking up at her from the ground, he said, "Get me a big towel as fast as you can."

He dodged a pickup truck and two cars, darting in front of them, smacking one's hood with the flat of his palm when it almost hit him. Samantha didn't even have time to draw another breath before he was across the street, vaulting the low wall the kids were crouching next to, huddled over a young man's prone form. From where she stood, she could see a rapidly growing pool of dark liquid coming from the boy's head.

Towel. He'd said big. She only had one really big towel,

and luckily, it was clean. She grabbed it, and raced out the door, down her stairs, and around the bagel shop. Luckily, there was no traffic coming and she pelted across the street, the white towel flapping behind her.

"Perfect." It must have been for a tenth of a second—less—that Hank's eyes met hers, but the warmth of approval she felt in that moment was unexpected. "Perfect."

From a pocket, he dug out a knife and slit the towel up the middle. He wadded one piece into a tight square and gave it to Samantha. "See that wound?"

How could she not? The boy's skull seemed to be dented, blood pouring from the cut. He must have hit it against the old anchor that rested on the sidewalk, a favorite of the tourists who often clustered like seagulls around it to take photos. The boy was unconscious but appeared to be breathing.

"Press it against the wound. Firmly."

A shiver shook Samantha, and then she stepped forward. "You got it." The boy was younger than he looked at a distance—he couldn't be more than fourteen. She kneeled and pressed the towel to his head.

"Careful not to jostle him." Hank wound the other half of the towel into a large U-shape and, reaching under her arm, fitted it around the boy's head and neck. "We're just stabilizing him until the ambulance gets here to transport him."

Samantha's head jerked up. "911. We have to call 911."

"Beckie already did it. That's what you said your name was, right? Beckie?" His hand on the boy's shoulder, Hank looked up at the girl who was crying the hardest, her phone still in her hand.

She nodded.

"Good girl. You did an amazing job. Hear those sirens?

That's the help you called. They're going to take good of him, thanks to you." To Samantha, he said, "A little more firmly. It's bleeding through a little. No, don't lift up to look. That's right. That's just perfect, Samantha."

Beckie spoke through her sobs, "Is he going to die?"

Hank gave a short laugh that did more to comfort Samantha than anything else could have. "Are you kidding me? No way. Good old Ralphie here's going to be fine. That is, if his mother doesn't kill him for ditching first period with you bozos. I have very little control over whether she kills him later or not."

One of the other boys who had been standing, frozen in place, gave a relieved and high-pitched giggle.

"That's perfect, Samantha," he said again.

But she *wasn't* doing it right. She could feel it. She could feel the heat of the boy's blood seeping through the towel, through her fingers. She was kneeling in the child's blood. She didn't know for sure if Hank could actually tell if the boy was going to be fine or not.

But then he said it again. "He'll be fine, Samantha. Because of you."

Her hands finally stopped shaking.

After Hank's coworkers on the ambulance left with the boy, and after the boy's mother had been tracked down by phone and directed to the emergency room where Hank continued to maintain he would be fine, after Hank had walked her back up the stairs, keeping his hand on the small of her back which Samantha was more grateful for than she'd ever admit, after he'd ushered her into the bathroom, telling her to take a hot shower, and that while she did that, he'd make her a cup of tea—did she like it black or with milk?—after she came out wrapped in her robe because her hands were shaking again, too much to button up her clean jeans, after all of that, when she looked into Hank's warm brown eyes, Samantha said, "You got the job."

"Well," said Hank, handing over her favorite yellow mug and then opening the French doors so a meowing Anchor could come in. "That's just fine, then."

CHAPTER 7

H ANK, IT TURNED out, was Jim Hind's height but not near his shape. The padded suit hung loosely at his hips where Jim was wider, but it was tight across the chest. It was itchy, too. And hot. Hank was already sweating, and he'd just put it on a few minutes before.

"You put on your cup, too, right?"

"You know it's embarrassing for a guy to be asked that, right?"

"Why?" Samantha was looking knock-out gorgeous again—all big green eyes and pink-cheeked, dressed simply in a black tank top and yoga pants. Her outfit formed to her curves in a way that would have made him uncomfortable if he *hadn't* been wearing a cup. Luckily, he was, and that was something of a buzz-kill.

"Because we're talking about my package here." He made a gesture with his hands toward his crotch. "My large, well-endowed, extremely precious package, might I add?" *Stay classy, Coffee.*

"Noted," Samantha said. "So it doesn't embarrass you to say *that*?"

"Nah," said Hank, glad he had the helmet on and that she couldn't see his eyes. "Simple truth doesn't make a man blush." He held out his arms, feeling a little like the Michelin Man in the get-up. "What now?"

"Now I see if I can make you scream like a little girl."

"Is that politically correct for you to say? I mean, given that you're in the job of training women?"

She shrugged and Hank was momentarily mesmerized by the way her bare shoulder rose and fell, the way the top of her breasts looked supported by that bra which was (thankfully) doing a bad job of holding her flatly down. "I train women. Not little girls."

"Because they scream like I'm about to."

"Exactly."

"Glad to know."

"Now, get onto the mat, okay?"

"Easy for you to say." Hank couldn't say with any certainty at all where his feet were going to land, and he was still trying to get the knack of seeing downward out the mesh eyeholes. "How am I supposed to move around in this at all?"

"You get the hang of it."

"How do you know? Do you ever have to wear this?"

She laughed and bounced on her toes. She was barefoot, which surprised him. Maybe she was going to go easy on him at first. That was fine, he'd take it.

"Yeah, I use it sometimes. Just to remember what it feels like."

Something about her voice was different. Darker on the last few words. She meant something more, but there was no way in hell he was going to ask her to explain if he couldn't really see her, couldn't meet her eyes with his own.

Briskly, Samantha said, "Okay. Are you ready?"

"Will you tell me again what you're going to do before you do it?"

"Just like you're getting a pap smear," she said.

"For God's sake," he groaned.

And then she kneed him in the nuts.

Hank dropped to his knees with a shout. "Hey! You said you'd warn me!" It didn't hurt, exactly, but the pressure of the blow had been so forcefully directed that it was more like it *should* have hurt.

"I lied." And she punched him in the head.

"Oh, my God," he groaned, lying on the mat as he faced the ceiling. "I don't know why I'm doing this."

She crouched, moving slowly around his body. It had only been two blows, but it felt like more.

"I think you're hitting my psyche. Is that possible?"

Samantha straightened. She put her hands on her hips and laughed out loud, such a pretty, happy sound that if he'd been able to figure out how to sit up, he would have, just to get a better look at her. "That's it!" she exclaimed. "You got it in two!"

"Good!" he said. "We're done for the day!"

"Just getting started, buddy. But yeah, that's exactly it. We don't fight fair here. You lie. You sneak. You attack. You make your prey feel like she's winning and just when she thinks she has you, you explode into motion again and pin her down until she cries. Then if she doesn't stop crying, you yell at her and let her up and knock her down again."

That got him sitting up. Hank yanked off his helmet. "No."

Samantha looked at him, her lips pressed into a firm line. "It's fine. Most people can't do it."

"I mean, no. Why do you do it this way?"

She walked away, across the room to a blue bag she'd

left on the floor. She got a water bottle out, and took a sip. Slowly, she came back toward him and without saying anything, offered him the bottle.

He drank.

"Because it's important that a woman knows she can do it."

"You need tricks for that? Lying? Doesn't seem fair to me." Hank stuck his legs out straight in front of him. The only thing he could see of his body that he recognized were his work boots, poking out from the bottom of the thick white suit.

Samantha pushed at the bridge of her nose as if she were pushing up the glasses she wasn't wearing. "You don't get it."

"Get what?"

She tilted her head and looked at him as if reassessing him. "No, I love that you don't."

"I'm missing something."

"I love that you've never had to think about this. That it doesn't exist in your mind. It also *infuriates* me that it doesn't." She dropped so that she was sitting on her knees, her legs folded beneath her. "Women don't get to make that choice. Whether something is fair or not. When a woman is attacked by a guy on the street, he doesn't ask politely whether she prefers to be hit in the face or punched in the gut."

Hank winced.

"When a woman wakes up to find a man she doesn't know kneeling over her in her own bed, holding her down as he rapes her while he holds a gun to her temple, she doesn't get a polite thank you when he's done. She gets hurt. She gets damaged, and most of the time she ends up damaged forever. *They're* the liars. They're the ones who usually win. But in here, *we* win. And we do it fair and square. When one of my students finishes a fight on top, she got there because she fought with her fists and knees and knuckles all the way there, not because she learned fancy moves with names she can't pronounce that don't do much more than help her abs."

She was making total sense, but he *hated* the fact that he might make a woman cry. On purpose.

In Darling Bay, they just didn't get the terrible crimes that big cities in California got. This wasn't San Francisco or Los Angeles. Darling Bay was just a sleepy northern town where their biggest problem was with the pot growers. Dealers tended to be armed as well as stoned, which wasn't a great combination. But apart from torching their own production shops with alarming regularity when the Feds got too close, creating fires that smelled like an outdoor music festival, the people up in the hills were mostly okay. Very few robberies were committed in Darling Bay, and the police force dealt with no more than one murder a year.

But rape happened. Again, not often, but it did happen. Hank had gone on a call earlier in the year in which a young woman, only eighteen, had been pulled off a running trail at the beach and dragged into the manzanita brush. The rapist wasn't a Darling Bay person—he been a tourist passing through. They'd never caught him. Hank thought of that girl sometimes, shaking so hard her teeth clattered, begging them to let her shower, Bonnie's arms around the girl before loading her carefully onto the ambulance, treating her as if she were a broken sand dollar. He wondered if she ever felt safe—really, truly safe. Even if she had a huge boyfriend who worked out—a guy who was a trained bodyguard and carried three guns and a knife—there would be times in her life when she'd be walking alone at night. There would be times she'd be in her kitchen, alone, her spatula poised over the stir-fry, wondering if the sound she'd just heard was the dog in the other room or someone breaking a window.

Hank hated the man who'd done it to her, who'd broken her like that. Who had, in many ways, ruined a large, important part of her whole *life*. Hank, who knew he would have had a hard time hating the very devil himself knowing that the guy was probably a pretty interesting drinking companion, hated that man who'd no doubt gone on to hurt other women, maybe without ever getting caught.

"Show me," he said. He cleared his throat roughly. "Show me how to help them."

Samantha threw her arms around him, catching him off guard. No blow here, just a hug that he could feel all the way through the padded suit. "Hug them first. Hug them when you meet them, and hug them before and after each session."

He hugged her back. Finally. Something he could probably get right.

CHAPTER 8

H ANK AMAZED HER.

He'd thrown himself into the training session, heart and soul. The first time she'd flown at him, he'd stumbled backward, protecting himself naturally with upraised arms. The second time, though? He'd fought back. She could tell he wasn't coming at her one hundred percent, and of course he wasn't. His whole job—his whole *life*—was about protecting people. Not pushing them, pinning them down, bringing them to a point where they could heal themselves.

But Hank had brought maybe eighty percent to their session. It was impressive.

Of course, she knew the moves by heart. She didn't have to think when she was ripping his arm away from her shoulder, using her lower body weight to flip him onto his back. He got her down once, but she could tell that he hadn't expected for her to start kicking as hard as she did. Yeah, he'd get used to that pretty soon. A woman's greatest strength was in her legs, and driving kicks at an attacker from a position on the ground was not only shocking but effective. Good. He'd reacted like a "normal" attacker, whatever that was, automatically retreating from her forward assault.

Breathing hard, she stood and signaled for him to take off his helmet.

"What? Was that wrong?" His face was flushed from exertion, and sweat dripped from the dark hair that hung at his eyes.

How could a man wearing a padded suit be so hot? She shouldn't be reacting to him like this.

It was his eyes. She had to ignore those dark smoky eyes, the way they seemed to ask something of her, something she couldn't put her finger on.

She leaned forward, putting her hands on her hips, taking a deep, delicious gulp of air. "No. You're doing awesome. Perfect."

"Good!" He frowned. "I mean, not good. Wait. Is that good?"

She laughed. "Yeah. It is. Wanna take that suit off?"

"Damn straight. I'm dying in here." He unsnapped and unzipped, stripping out of the suit. He'd worn what she'd told him to—a T-shirt, shorts, and his heavy work boots.

The thing was, Samantha hadn't thought about the fact that she'd get to see him in a whole lot of his glory. Those legs, for example. His considerable height was all in those legs, those extremely muscled limbs. "Do you ride a bike?"

He looked confused. Naturally. "A motorcycle?"

"Nah," she said. "I hate motorcycles. I meant a bicycle. Your..." She gestured at his legs, feeling suddenly very young and stupid. "You have a lot of muscles."

Hank grinned. "Well, thanks. I think you must just be impressed by my black uniform socks tucked into my boots. Now, if you don't mind, I've got to go..."

Take off the cup. Of course he did.

"And then I need a shower like a rookie on his first house fire."

"Yeah, yes. I can't thank you enough. You did great." She handed him the water bottle, and somehow, watching his Adam's apple bob as he swallowed seemed more intimate than anything else they'd done. He'd manhandled her in the training, and she'd sat on top of his body, her face next to his ear. At one point she'd had him lie on top of her—the way they did with the students who had a history of being trapped by a man in bed—and it had been all business. He'd been the attacker.

But now, the combination of the plane of his jaw, shiny with sweat, the stubble around his mouth, and the way his fingers accidentally brushed hers as he handed back the bottle made something inside of Samantha quake. "You did great," she said again.

"I want to take you out."

"Good grief." He was so *blunt*. She put the cap back on the bottle, tightening it so much she probably wouldn't be able to get it off later. "What?"

"I need to tell you that. I want to work with you, professionally, yes. I think what you told me about the way we can help your students is one of the best things I've heard in years. If I can help them protect themselves, to make them feel safe, then that's truly admirable. But damn, Samantha. I want to kiss you so bad I can't stand it and since I'm never going to do it while we're training, I've got to get you somewhere else to try my luck."

There was a half-smile on Hank's face. A sweet smile.

And at the same time it was so sexy her toes curled.

"I can't. We can't. Not if we're going to work together."

"Okay. I quit."

Honestly surprised, Samantha said, "No! I need you."

"Then go out with me."

She twisted the bottle in her hands. In about one second she'd start stripping the paper from it with nervous fingers, the way she used to strip beer bottles sitting at the bar.

He continued, "Just once. Just give it a shot. It's probably a bad idea, just like it was back then."

It hadn't been a bad idea. She'd just been an idiot, that was all. But time went on, and life changed, and people like Hank stayed good and sweet and unspoiled. "Hank," she said slowly, "I hurt you back then. I don't want to do that again."

He barked a laugh. "Are you still worried about that?"

Samantha curled her fingers tighter around the bottle. "Yeah. Maybe."

"Honey," he drawled. "I'm not talking about falling in love with you. I've done that, and honestly, you cured me of the whole love thing, way back when. I'm just thinking about what your mouth might taste like."

Samantha couldn't help it—she gasped. Then she said, "One date. Just one. Tomorrow night."

"What do you want to do?"

Without thinking, she said, "Something risky. Something scary. Something I've never done."

"Night kayaking?"

"Done it."

"Hang gliding from Bogel Peak?"

She laughed. "In the dark?"

"Maybe not." He paused. "Have you ever been rock climbing?"

"No! I've always wanted to go, though. I just hadn't gotten around to it. There's that new climbing gym in Eureka, right?"

Hank nodded and finished hanging the padded suit inside out so it could air. "I'll pick you up at seven."

"In the seventy-two Mustang?"

"You know my car?"

"You kidding? I saw you drive up. Is that stock black?"

Hank nodded in surprise. "She's my baby."

"Well, if you ever need a babysitter..." She looked slightly embarrassed. "Anyway. See you tomorrow."

Hank started to leave and then said, "Almost forgot." He turned and wrapped her in a hug. It felt different this time, without the padding. With the desired kiss burning between them. She could smell his deodorant, green and crisp, and the scent underneath it, good clean, well-earned sweat.

And then he left, leaving Samantha standing alone in the middle of the padded mat. She dropped to a cross-legged position. She touched her lips.

She felt her mouth stretch into a grin.

CHAPTER 9

DOWNSTAIRS IN THE bagel shop, Samantha was pulling her normal Thursday morning shift. She wasn't good at being in the back, making the bagels. She'd tried, and every single time she pulled them out of the water or moved them to the oven, she'd burned a finger or wrist to the blister point. She wasn't allowed in the kitchen anymore, and Johannes made her use the bagel guillotine to slice every bagel. "No knife for you."

"Come on, Johannes. I'm smart enough not to cut my finger off." But secretly, Samantha was relieved. She *was* clumsy everywhere but the training mat. Although she was a good cook, she didn't do well with knives and she probably would have damaged herself permanently if he'd wanted her to cut a gajillion bagels every morning. The guillotine was fast and safe, and it gave a satisfying thunk every time she *shoonked* the bread in two.

The line in the well-lit bagel shop that morning had been constant, with moms with strollers in tow and kids coming in before school. The girls always ordered the fancy, sweet ones—light fluffed strawberry cream cheese on cinnamon bagels—and the boys ordered bagels with scrambled eggs. Samantha's favorite customers were the older men who spent the day rambling in and out of all the businesses on First Street. They started early, at Mabel's Cafe, for thick black coffee. Around nine, they'd wheel into the bagel shop, ordering poppyseed or everything bagels, toasted dark. They never used anything but the traditional thick cream cheese. They liked their coffee black and she'd never seen even one of them drinking water.

Her favorite was Gus Treat. He was of indeterminate age, somewhere north of eighty. He'd been a career military pilot, and he still put a lot of energy into looking neat and trim. Today he wore a dark blue shirt with matching pants, the pressed lines clean and sharp. His face was shiny from his close shave.

"Morning, Gus. The regular?" Samantha had learned early in the food industry that nothing made a customer happier than making their order before they asked for it. It made them feel special, which was good, because Gus was.

He nodded and reached in his back pocket for his wallet.

"How's it going?" she asked.

"Fine, just fine." He reached for a mug to help himself to the coffee on the counter. "Gotta ask you a favor, girlie. Got a minute?"

Samantha took off her apron. She loved talking to Gus. He had more gossip at his fingertips than anyone else in town, and no one loved to speculate on other people's business more than he did. She didn't know most of the people he talked about so she wasn't very invested, but his chatter was friendly. Welcome.

"Hey, Johannes, I'm going to take a quick break, okay?

The salt bagel is for Mark, okay, and the poppyseed that's in the toaster is for Gus. But I'll get it for him when it's ready."

Johannes nodded and took her place.

Gus had taken a seat at the small bar that ran along the window, facing the pier.

Samantha pulled up the stool next to Gus. Outside the window, a blue boat with a red furled sail chugged by under motor power. Through the glass she could just hear its thump as it hit the dock's bumper. She touched the window with one finger, knowing she'd be the one to clean off the smudge later.

"What's up, Gus?"

"Who's the boy?"

Samantha pretended ignorance. Sometimes it was best. "The boy who fell off the wall yesterday out there?" She pointed. "I didn't know him, but he's fine."

"The other boy. The firefighter."

"Oh, him."

Gus shot her a look and then peered over her shoulder. "My bagel's done."

Samantha got up and took out Gus's bagel just before it burned and slathered it thickly with cream cheese. She slid it in front of him and sat down again.

"So. A fireman, huh?"

Samantha smiled and traced a star pattern with her thumbnail on the napkin. When she'd dated Hank so long ago, she'd asked him what lengths he'd go to in order to become a firefighter. He'd said he would do anything—absolutely anything, short of hurting someone—and she hadn't understood that passion, his drive. She'd only had one motivating force back then, to *go*, to *do*, to *be*. She'd wanted to live fast and hard. She'd wanted to get all the things done that her mother had always wanted to do but hadn't had enough time to get done before she died. For her mother, Samantha had to travel, to cross the Pacific and Atlantic, she had to be brave, she had to push herself. Unfortunately, she'd pushed herself in the wrong direction, and had ended up with not only the wrong men but the wrong habits.

"What was your father like?" Gus asked unexpectedly.

"Steady. Reliable. We weren't that much alike except that he got obsessed with things. For him, it was mostly strawberries. His farm. Once he made up his mind he wanted something, he went after it like a dog after a chicken bone."

"For you it was booze."

After a while, yes. She hadn't seen it coming—she thought she'd been chasing adventure in her mother's name, in her honor, but what she'd really been doing was chasing a kind of drunken peace.

That peace just never stayed. "Yeah."

"And then it was fighting? That training stuff you do for girls?"

"Women," she corrected him. "Yeah."

"And now him."

She narrowed her eyes at her neighbor. "I'm not *chasing* him. Actually, the opposite. What do you do upstairs? Send Anchor out to spy on me?"

Gus shrugged. "That cat comes in handy. And that's what I wanted to ask you, actually. I'm going out of town for a week to Costa Rica, can you watch him?"

"Fancy. Of course."

"Might not come back."

"Nor should you," Samantha said. "Not if you don't want to."

"Slow down," Gus said.

Confused, Sam said, "Excuse me?"

"Not about my cat. But about everything else. You move too fast."

Samantha smiled. "Are you accusing me of being the town hussy? Should I be offended?"

Gus shook his head impatiently. "All of you kids, with your phones and tablets and cordless whosiwhatsits, you're all moving too fast. Sit on the porch with that boy. What's the sunset *for* if not to watch it with someone?"

Glancing over her shoulder, catching Johannes's harried look, Samantha said, "What if I like going this fast?"

Gus lifted his coffee mug to his mouth, slow as fog. "You're going to miss something, girlie. Or someone. Take your time. Make sure you don't fall off the cliff you're always in danger of jumping from."

Spontaneously, she kissed his smooth-shaven cheek. "I hear you, friend. And I'm going to sit on my porch and watch the sunset, just for you."

"Maybe with that fireman."

"Maybe," she granted before standing. "Leave Anchor's food by my door, okay?"

CHAPTER 10

IT WASN'T A good idea.

He knew it wasn't. Hank shouldn't have said it.

Rock climbing.

But heck, it was exciting and scary and what better thing to do to inspire trust between two people?

Okay, he could think of one other thing, and he was trying super damn hard not to go there in his mind...

He knocked on the glass pane of her window that was still loose.

"It's open," he heard her call from inside.

Of course it was.

"I'll just be a second, I'm sorry, I lost track of time." Her voice floated out the cracked bathroom door. He caught a brief glance of her in a sliver of mirror—she was pulling back her hair into a ponytail, and for one second, he imagined pulling out the rubber band, running his fingers through that incredible mane of hers. "Make yourself comfortable."

"Take your time." Sticking his hands in his pockets, he moved to the French doors and pulled back the curtain. The early winter night had dropped, and the lights in the harbor glittered at him. Yeah, he loved his house, sure, and it was awesome that it was a ten minute walk to the waterline, but this view was something else. Turning, he brought his gaze to the inside of her apartment again.

It was different at night. Softer. One lamp glowed in the corner, lighting a patch of sofa that looked just right to sink into with a book. At the top of her walls, running along all of them, were white twinkle lights. They provided the only other light, and they glowed gently.

A white extension cord caught his eye. Oh, *hell,* no.

Hank crouched. He tugged the cord and watched the strand of lights above his head bounce slightly.

Samantha came out of the bathroom. She looked different than she had yesterday at the community center— her eyes were smokier, smudged with a dark brown. Her lips were soft pink and glossy.

Hank had never wanted anything more than to kiss that gloss away.

Instead, he said, "You've got a fire hazard here, ma'am." He lifted the white cord as high as he could to show her.

"You sound very professional, sir."

He touched an imaginary hat. "At your service. But really, you can't do this."

She looked up at the white lights. "Seems I am, though. I don't have enough outlets in this ancient apartment."

"There are ways to fix that," he said. "Safer ways than this. Seriously, how much did you pay for this cord? Five bucks?"

She looked chagrined. "I think I got it at the hardware store on sale for ninety-nine cents."

"No. Uh-uh," he said. "Didn't your mom ever teach you that you get what you pay for?"

Samantha shook her head. "My mom was the biggest cheapskate that ever lived. She not only washed and reused our sandwich bags, she asked the next door neighbor for her kids' bags, because she noticed they didn't do the same thing."

"Maybe she was being environmentally responsible."

"Nah. She just liked to save money. I kind of like it, too. It's fun to make new things out of old."

"Were you two close?"

Samantha's face softened. "The closest."

"She's..."

"She died when I was a kid."

"I'm sorry."

"Me, too. She was only forty-five."

"Too damn young."

"Yeah. You? Your parents?"

Hank said, "Both died when I was twelve. Both of cancer."

"Bad year."

"Really bad year."

Samantha pushed those invisible glasses up on her nose. "Anyway."

"Do me a favor and get better extension cords?"

Her look was patient. "Look. I'll try to remember to do that, but I tend to live life on the edge a little bit. I drink milk that's expired, I light my own pilot on the stove, and I've never had trouble with extension cords or people breaking into my apartment. Until you, that is."

"You light your own pilot?" No one did that anymore. It was hot.

"I smelled gas the other day and I hesitated a little, but I figured if the other pilots were on, the house was in no danger of exploding."

"You *smelled* natural gas? You sure it was just your pilot?"

"Hank?" She touched his arm, and he completely forgot what they were talking about.

"Yeah?"

"Let's go climb a rock."

CHAPTER 11

AT THE CLIMBING gym, Samantha proved to be an eager pupil. Hank enjoyed the feeling of teaching after being her student the day before.

It would have been normal if she'd been a little hesitant when she first looked up at the rock walls. Six stories overhead, people hoisted themselves, using nothing more than their body weight to scale the height. Ropes dangled from the very highest heights, and everywhere, men and women in harnesses glided and soared.

But instead of looking worried as she craned her neck to look up, she seemed to glow.

There she was, the girl who taught him never to trust in love, looking almost as young and even more beautiful as she had back then. And *damn*, the woman looked good in a harness. The canvas straps cupped and outlined her rear end in a way that might be classified as dangerous. It was a good thing he was hoping to just have a physical fling with her to get her out of his system, for once and for all. Because how could a man hope to keep up with a woman like her in the long run?

Men didn't keep up with Samantha Rowe. That's why she was still single. And that was why, when this whatever it was ended, he'd be ready to get into a good relationship. A healthy one.

Samantha pulled the rope tighter around her waist, touching the knot at her bellybutton with her fingers. "Did I do this one right?"

The first time she'd done the figure eight knot, she'd done it wrong. It was that kind of mistake that killed people, and Hank had a hard time slowing his breathing, looking at it.

But this time, on only her second try, she'd gotten it exactly right. She held her arms out. "Check me!"

"Yes."

They'd spent the first hour with Raul, the manager. Although Hank was experienced enough he could have taught Samantha all the rope moves, all the safety information, he'd left that to Raul. What if he got distracted by something Samantha said or did and forgot to show her something important? He wouldn't take that chance. Besides, it never hurt for anyone to get a brush-up.

Samantha struggled with her first attempt going up. It was never as easy as it looked, and everyone found that out in their own way. Those rock handholds looked as if they were in reasonable places, but once your body was on the wall, it was different. The blue 5.6 grade you thought would be simple would turn out to require taking a toe-jump or a spiderman-stretch.

"Take," she yelled at him from only about four feet up. This was the signal that she was going to come off the wall, that in a second he'd be supporting her weight on the leveraged rope.

"I've got you."

Hank had to hand it to her—he'd heard a lot of women, and men, for that matter, fall off the wall their first time with a sharp scream that sent grins around the climbing gym. But she didn't yell.

Instead, when the rope caught her, leaving her dangling in midair, she laughed. She whooped with delight, and when he let her down to the ground, when her feet made contact, she was still laughing.

"That was the best thing ever!" She stood straight, brushing the chalk off her hands, leaving white handprints on her leggings. "I want to do it again, but I can't. My arms need a break. My *fingers*. I had no idea it would be that hard to hang on."

The delight in her voice was almost something palpable, something he wanted to hang at his waist with his chalk bag and extra carabiners. "It's fun."

"It's not simply *fun*. It's *amazing*." She held out her hands, already red and scratched. "I am *so* badass."

She was. But Hank had a sneaking suspicion she'd been born that way. "My turn."

Samantha, undoing her rope, looked up at him with a sudden hesitation. "Are you sure?"

"Yeah."

"You're big."

"Yeah." He made his own figure eight knot.

"Really big. I mean, what do you weigh?"

"A little over two hundred."

"You're sure this whole leverage thing will actually work?"

Hank had seen ten-year-old kids hoisting their adult fathers. "It's going to work."

They checked each other for safety. She was good. Thorough. She'd listened to Raul, and she was bringing back every part of the lesson, not forgetting a thing. He moved to the wall and said, "On belay."

She responded correctly, "Belay on." She would do well. He wasn't surprised.

"Climbing."

"Climb on."

He started up the wall. This was the best part, whether he was indoors or out. Some people liked the coming down part, that quick rush of falling down the hill, supported by the rope and nothing else. But Hank liked the feeling of using his body and his brain together. He liked the fact that it was harder than anything else. When you were running, you could shut your brain off and just do it. Kayaking, same thing. But every single second that you were climbing, you were thinking.

"Nice view, Coffee," she called from two stories below.

His hands suddenly got sweaty, and he fumbled for the chalk.

Usually on this particular grade, he could get to the top in less than ten minutes. But this time, it was proving harder. Knowing she was watching was part of it. It made his nerves jangle. But more than that, for the first time in a long time, he wasn't that interested in being on the wall, making it to the top. It was more fun, being on the ground with her.

"Take," he called.

"What?" she yelled back. "Am I supposed to be holding on to the rope right now?"

He swung his head around and stared down at her in disbelief.

"Just kidding! Go ahead!" She laughed.

It wasn't goddamn funny.

Hank came off the wall. She controlled his descent at a

good rate—not so fast the bottom of his stomach dropped out and not so slow that he'd get bored dangling.

But no matter how perfect his descent was, it didn't take an iota away from his fury.

"That was amazing," she said, her cheeks pink with excitement. "You went so high! I couldn't believe it!"

He clawed at the knot and ripped off the rope. "We're done. Untie."

"What?"

"Do it. We're leaving." His hands shook, not from the difficulty of the climb but from the white-hot rage that pulsed through his body.

"Oh, *no*. Is it because I teased you? I was just joking. I'm so sorry! I never let go of the rope. I wouldn't do that. Raul scared the hell out of me with his lesson."

If Hank had been in a mood to give her any credit, she did look horrified. But he wasn't. "Just take off the rope."

"But..."

"Change into your street clothes. I'll pay and meet you at the car."

He'd been planning on taking her to the Crab's Claw. White tablecloths, red napkins, the kind of place a woman liked to be wined and dined, if anything he read in the Yelp reviews were right. He'd planned on plying her with two glasses of wine, and then he'd planned on walking to her door and kissing the breath out of her in front of it.

"I'll take you home."

"Wait, you're punishing me for—"

"Go change," he growled before stalking away from her, leaving her open-mouthed.

He wasn't *punishing* her.

But outside, leaning against the Mustang, he could admit it. He *was* punishing her. It wasn't fair—she didn't know his history. There'd be no reason for her to. It was his history, not hers.

She came out of the gym, her sports clothes in the small green bag she'd brought. "Are you still mad at me?"

"Yep."

"Well, you're being an ass."

Wait a minute. That wasn't what he expected. "Excuse me?"

"I made a mistake. And it wasn't even like I made a safety error because I never let go of the rope. It was totally wrong to joke about it, but I apologized. There's no good reason for you to act like this, and I'm starting to think you're right to end this date, because I'm not that big on going on dates with jerks."

She was right. But no way was he going to let her know that. Hank didn't get upset often, but his grandmother Maureen always said, "when you do, it's atomic. And it's always for a good reason."

It *was* for a good reason, but it wasn't one he wanted to talk about.

Maybe it was just easier to let her think he was a gigantic jerkwad and drive her home.

"Let's go, then." He opened her car door. She shook her head but got in. Right before he closed the door, she looked up at him with those clear green eyes and said, "You're fired. Again."

CHAPTER 12

I T WAS THE only thing she could do. She *had* to fire him.

But maybe she could have waited until he'd gotten her back to the apartment.

He slid into the driver's seat, dangerously quiet. He started the car and pulled out, driving smoothly. No fast revs, no quick turns, no slam of brakes. Anger pulsed from his body.

No *way* was she letting someone who could get this mad so fast near her students.

Outside her passenger-side window, the world passed quietly. At the turn on First Street, the marina came into view, the lights on the pier burning dimly through the fog that had rolled in like a thick blanket of dark wool. The red Closed sign glowed in the bagel shop window. Above it, she could see her white twinkle lights gleaming against her windows.

"You shouldn't leave those on when you leave."

"Fine." She wasn't going to argue with him. She just wanted him to pull into the parking lot and let her out. The disappointment was thick in the back of her throat. She'd been strangely excited about this date, and now she even more strangely let down. Yeah, she'd screwed up. But this anger of his was apparently coiled like a rattler under a wood pile, just as unexpected and twice as unpleasant.

"You shouldn't leave those on when you're home, now that I think of it. Not till you get a better extension cord, a heavy duty one with a surge protector."

She turned in her seat as she unsnapped the seatbelt. Facing him, Samantha said, "I hate to break it to you, buddy, but you don't get to give advice on my life."

"As a member of the local fire protection district—"

"What are you going to do, write me a ticket?"

"You have to—"

"Oh, screw you, Hank." Angry at herself for having that ridiculous tiny little hope, she pushed open the heavy door.

"Wait." His voice was low.

Samantha owed him nothing. She didn't have to wait. But she gave him the second. If he was going to ask for his job back...

"I killed someone."

She turned toward him again, one leg out of the car, one leg in. "Are you kidding me?"

"Wish I was." Hank leaned his head back on the vinyl headrest and looked in the rearview mirror as if the car was still moving. "Right before I graduated. Not long after you left, actually."

"What happened?" Samantha's voice was still curt and she'd lost all ability to figure out what to feel next.

"We were climbing in Colorado, on a trip with some other guys in my paramedic training. We were trying a cliff face none of us had done before."

"He was going up, I was belaying. His hand slipped at

the same time that the foothold he was using gave way. We hadn't double checked our knots. The rope slid through my hands, and I tried to grab it, but it was like I was moving in slow motion and the rope just twisted away from me so fast. There was nothing I could do." Hank's voice was even. Calm. It was as if he were relaying a story about someone else, someone he didn't know very well. "He twisted in the air when his foot hit the wall and he landed on his back, snapping his neck. I knew he was dead even before I took the twelve steps to get to him."

Samantha's breath caught in her throat. "It wasn't your—"

"Oh, it was totally my fault. Our fault, but I was the one who lived, so it's all mine. I was cocky, and going too fast, and I hadn't used the right protocol. I wanted to be a *firefighter*. I wanted to protect people, and I'd done it wrong and killed someone instead. There are rules for everything, everywhere. Protocol for safety in firefighting, in stocking grocery shelves, even in relationships, for cripe's sakes. And I'd ignored protocol."

Softly, she said, "What was his name?"

Hank glanced at her. "Jimmy. His name was Jimmy."

She didn't remember a Jimmy in the group of people that had hung around with Hank back then.

"He was a redhead. The one who insisted on riding his skateboard everywhere, even if I offered him a ride."

"Oh!" She remembered Jimmy. He'd given her a piece of Bazooka bubblegum and they'd laughed together at the comic inside the wrapper. That day in the cafeteria of their junior college felt like it had happened last week. She didn't recall anything else about him, but she remembered clearly how hard he'd laughed at that silly comic strip. "He gave me gum once."

"Bazooka?" Hank's voice was heartbreaking, hopeful and desolate at the same time.

"Yeah."

"His mom had huge bowls of that gum out at the funeral. I still can't even smell bubblegum."

"I'm so sorry." Samantha wanted to touch him, to put her hand on his arm, but she suspected that if she moved even an inch, he'd snap. His body was rigid, as if he were holding himself together with rebar.

"No. I'm the one who's sorry." He looked steadily forward through the glass. "My behavior tonight was unforgivable."

"Nothing's unforgivable."

Now he looked at her, and his eyes were dark with despair. "Didn't you hear the story I just told you? Once you kill your buddy, there's nothing you can do to get him back. That's pretty much the very definition of the word."

It wasn't, but it didn't do to tell him that right now.

Samantha twisted in her seat, drawing up her legs so that she was half-kneeling. A gust of wind pushed the car door closed behind her.

Without thinking about it, worried that if she did she would stop, Samantha leaned forward and put her lips on Hank's. For one long second, their mouths rested against each other's. Samantha didn't hear him breathing. She certainly wasn't. His lips were firm, warm. Just the right shape.

Then, with a jerk, he pulled back. "What the—"

Awesome. "Sorry." Maybe if Samantha backed straight out as fast as she could, she could get out of the Mustang with one percent of her dignity left. She'd gladly leave the other ninety-nine percent hanging in shreds behind her, if it meant she could go upstairs and push her head under her pillow. "Okay, then..."

And then Hank came out of his seat. At her. In a split second, both his hands were wrapped around the back of her head, and he was pulling her to him, his mouth hot and demanding against hers. She pushed back against him—it was a war as to who could kiss the hardest, and Samantha would do anything to win. And she'd do anything to lose.

Wrapping her arms around his neck, she moved forward, bringing her knee over the middle console. His tongue tangled with hers, stroking her at first and then plundering her mouth. He tasted like mint and, faintly, of something sweet, something else that was all him. She wanted more, *more*. She wanted to kiss his neck, she wanted to nip the skin just under his chin, but she couldn't tear her mouth from his for even a second. Every time she tried, he kissed her harder. Deeper.

She leaned her upper body against his, and his whole seat shot backward as he hit the release. She grinned against his lips and brought her other leg across so that she was straddling him on the front seat. His hands cupped her buttocks and she tilted so that her jeans pressed into his. She could feel his hardness under the material, hot against her thigh, and she pulled away for a split second to meet his eyes.

Hank's gaze was so dark he looked like the devil. He looked like her salvation, too.

He pulled her head down to his again for another kiss. She was liquid inside, quaking with the need. What his tongue was doing to hers, the way it made her writhe against him, out here in the parking lot for all to see—she wanted that tongue to go other places. *All* her places.

"Come inside."

"Honey," he drawled, pulling her hips against his again, "I like to use protection."

She laughed. "Inside the apartment. Please."

He sobered suddenly, pushing his forehead against hers. "I can't."

"Why?" She ran her fingers up the line of his jaw, under his ear, reveling in the strength of the muscle she felt there. She put her thumb to his bottom lip and he groaned.

"You just fired me," he managed, lifting his hand to hers. "For the second time."

She slipped his finger into her own mouth and sucked for a second. She felt him get even harder. "You're unfired."

"That's emotional whiplash. I should sue or something."

"Then we'll call it even," she said. "You got mad at me, way too mad, but now I know why. Let's split the difference and go inside where you can take off all my clothes."

He laughed, but it sounded choked. "You are the hottest thing on two legs."

It wasn't the most romantic line she'd ever been handed, but she'd take it. He was a firefighter, not a poet. "Thanks. I like your legs, too. And I like this." She tugged on his belt, drawing his hips to hers again. She leaned over and kissed him. When she came up for air, she said, "I like that, too. I know, we'll do this a different way. Come upstairs, and I'll take off all *your* clothes."

This time it was a real laugh. But he twisted, putting her away from him with a smooth lift and turn. "I'm not going to take advantage of you like that."

She flopped back into her seat with a groan. "*I want you to.*" That was the whole point.

"Samantha." He scooted his seat forward again and looked her straight in the eye. "I want you. Honestly, I'd love to try to get you out of my system."

Samantha smiled. She felt the same way and liked his honesty.

Hank went on, "I reckon you felt just how much I want you. But I can't."

"Why?" No, she didn't get this. "Yeah, you got angry, but—"

"That." He gripped the steering wheel. "That's the problem. I've been trying to make it up to Jimmy since the day it happened by being the guy he wanted to be—we both, we were so into being firemen. Protecting. Saving. Instead, I scared a woman. I scared you. You were right to fire me." He reached forward and touched her cheek. His hand was warm.

It made her feel safe while doing absolutely nothing to relieve the feeling of need deep inside her.

"I have to go."

She growled in the back of her throat. Then she jammed open the car door again, kicking at it with her foot like she would an assailant. "Fine. But I need you at the community center at nine a.m., day after tomorrow. You said you were off, right?"

Hank nodded, his eyes narrowing. "But..."

"Look. I need your help, Hank."

As she slammed the Mustang's heavy door behind her, she felt a grim satisfaction. At least, putting it that way, he might show up.

But it was going to do nothing for the fire she still felt inside her body, low and deep. The firefighter had started that flame—that was the problem. No one but him could help her put it out.

CHAPTER 13

O F *COURSE* HANK'S grandmother would come by at eight in the morning. Hank hadn't been able to sleep, not even after he got up and went for a run in the middle of the night, battling his way through the freezing night-time air, his lungs heaving with something he hoped would turn to tiredness. He'd come back and gotten into bed, and instead of dropping into sleep, his head had spun with thoughts of her.

The taste of her.

The feel of the nape of her neck in his hand. The way her body molded to his, the way when he kissed her she responded with the perfect heat before she took it even higher.

No fire he'd ever fought, not even the one at the magnesium plant seven years before, had ever burned hotter than she did against him.

After a cold shower followed by a hundred push-ups, he'd finally started getting tired. He dropped off to sleep sometime after five a.m., so when the doorbell shrilled, Hank shoved his head under the pillow and cursed.

The doorbell rang again. Gramma Maureen had a signature way of doing it—she pushed the button once, quickly, and then, always unsure it had rung inside since her hearing was going, she'd lean on it for a long minute. Before his old dog Samson had died, that particular method of ringing the doorbell had driven his dog right over the edge. He'd howl for a good ten minutes after Maureen left, scared that she'd come back and do it again.

Get up.

The doorbell rang again. There was no ignoring Maureen.

"Dear boy." Maureen, wearing a red knitted sweater with the image of a large banana embroidered into the front, a black skirt that looked frayed at the edges, and big clompy black men's shoes, lifted herself to her very tiptoes to kiss Hank's cheek. Hank still had to bend down to receive it. "Look at you. You look like you just rolled out of bed."

"I did."

As if she hadn't heard him—and perhaps she hadn't—Maureen went on. "But it's past eight in the morning—"

"Two past."

"And a boy like you doesn't oversleep."

Sometimes Hank wondered how old Maureen thought he was. She'd treated him the exact same way since she'd taken over raising him when his parents had died. She treated him like a child who needed to be coddled, while at the same time, maintaining an implicit faith in him to do everything the way a good man would.

It was always good to see her, of course. If it didn't happen to be eight-oh-two in the dang morning.

She bustled through the living room, tut-tutting at yesterday's paper he'd left strewn on the couch cushions. Somehow she managed to balance her red basket and cup of coffee while still gathering the sections of newspaper under her arm.

"You look like Little Red Riding Hood, with your sweater and your basket."

His grandmother humphed. "She didn't have such a gorgeous sweater." She touched the embroidered banana proudly. "Did I show you this one?"

"You did. I hadn't noticed that you'd used glitter yarn for the banana, though."

"Best invention of the nineties."

He didn't bother filling her in that a couple of decades had come and gone since the nineties. She still lived alone, just four blocks away, and while she lived on his grandfather's life insurance, she made her spending money by teaching knitting classes. She'd somehow gained fame through knitting; Hank didn't know how she'd pulled that off, but she had tourists coming to town expressly to learn her yarn embroidery techniques. Maureen enjoyed nothing more than creating sweaters that most of the world would call ugly, and wearing them so proudly that he'd seen people in Mabel's Cafe offer to buy her sweaters right off her back.

His grandmother had to take over being mother and father right at the point he'd been headed into his awful teen years, and she'd done a fine job with limited means. Hank loved her more than he loved anyone in the world. And she loved him even more fiercely. He knew that. He felt it in her grip when she hugged him.

And yet that didn't ever, *ever* get him off the hook.

"Heard you were a butthead in Eureka yesterday," Maureen said.

Hank groaned and reached for the coffee pot. "That's it. I'm moving."

Maureen set her knitting basket on the table with a clatter and pulled out her needles. The sweater-in-progress was a toxic green-yellow. "Don't bother with coffee. I had mine hours and hours ago."

"I'm sure you did. This is for me."

"So, what made you so mad you canceled a whole date?"

Hank turned, the pot still in his hand, and stared. He could imagine that Maureen could glean info that included who he'd been on a date with, and perhaps what they'd done, but the fact that he'd canceled it? That he'd been a jerk of the first degree?

"Did you also know that we had sex in the Mustang?"

Maureen waved her hand. "Don't you try to shock me, young man. I know you smooched and then she left in a huff."

There were eyes in the trees, spies *everywhere*. Really, he had enough in savings that he could run off to Mexico and be pretty damn comfortable for at least a few years before he had to figure out a next step. He should just go. But damn, if he'd packed a bag, Maureen would have heard it through the grapevine and would probably show up within minutes of him zipping the suitcase.

"Do you happen to know where I left my spare key?" It was a smart-alec question. His spare hadn't been on his hook for the last month, and he couldn't figure out what he'd done with it. There was no reason for Maureen to know where it had gone, though.

She lifted a ring of keys out of her basket and jingled it. "I took it."

Didn't that just figure. "Why? You already had one, and you always ring the doorbell anyway."

"So I could have Eva come in and clean. She needed a key."

"That's what I hire Rosamunde to do. Every two weeks." Hank was terrible at house-cleaning and he knew it. Rosamunde was the daughter of Eva, Maureen's longtime best friend.

"She's terrible at the baseboards. Eva's better."

"You're too old for the baseboards. For that matter, so's Eva." Hank hated to think about someone his grandmother's age hunched over, wiping the corners of his rooms.

"Ah, I'm just messing with you," said Maureen. "Rosamunde's great. I just wanted a key so we could watch your cable TV when you're at work."

"And again, what about your key?"

She suddenly became extra invested in something her fingers were doing.

"Gramma?"

"Oh, all right. I dropped it off the pier."

"Excuse me?"

"I needed something to throw at a seagull that had taken one of my stitch markers."

Hank shook his head. Sometimes he thought it would be easier talking to a three-year-old than Maureen, even though her faculties were still sharp as her pointy needles.

The pot had almost a full cup of coffee in it now, and he poured it into his mug. He couldn't wait any longer for it. He *needed* it.

"So, Gramma, what's up this morning? Besides knowing more about my life than I do, apparently."

"I need to tell you not to see that girl anymore."

Hank blinked. "Samantha?"

"Who else are you seeing, Madonna?"

Someday he'd introduce her to a current pop artist. "I appreciate your concern."

"But I should butt out." Maureen clicked her needles and her fingers were moving so fast he could barely tell what she was doing. "I hear you. But I'm not concerned with what you think about this one."

"You never are."

Maureen pressed the tip of a needle to her chest and took a breath that would inflate a blimp. "You wound my *heart* when you say that. Right here is where I feel it. In the middle of the night, all I can think about is my grandson and his happiness. What did I do to deserve—" She reminded Hank of an opera singer, her chest heaving with emotion.

"Before you get all wound up like that, can you please do a man a favor and get to the point?"

Maureen deflated and cheered up. "Okay. Look. That girl's no good. Never has been. There. I want great-grand-kids someday and I don't want a junkie to give birth to some meth-addled crackbaby."

"*What?*"

"You know what I mean. Dump her. You can't trust a girl like her. And Eva says there's a new waitress at Mabel's, and she's just the kind of girl you like, all skinny and blond."

"I like a brunette with curves." Samantha had perfect curves, made for speed.

"You do not."

"That's like telling me I don't like pickles."

"But you *do* like pickles. You love them!"

"I know. But if you told me I didn't like them, it wouldn't make me like them less. And there's nothing wrong with Samantha Rowe."

"She's not good enough for you."

Actually, it was just the opposite. Samantha Rowe was way too good for a guy like him.

Hank waited. There would be more. There always was. He watched as Maureen thought—he could almost see the wheels turning inside her head. Gradually, her face dropped, her eyes getting bigger and wetter. Her mouth sagged into sadness, and her lower lip wobbled. Man. His grandmother was good.

Her voice trembled as she said, "It's just that I'm not getting any younger, my darling. I don't expect to be around for my next birthday—"

"Are you dying currently? Because your birthday is in three weeks," Hank pointed out helpfully.

"I know that," snapped Maureen, breaking character. "Look. Is it so terrible if I want my future great-grandchildren to be healthy and happy?"

"How about your current grandson? Do you care about him?"

"You know you're my life."

It wasn't true. Her life was her knitting and the bridge club that was more like a sorority and her three cats and about a million charity projects. "I love you, too."

"Will you dump her for me?" Maureen batted her eyelashes, and Hank noticed something different about them. Something odd.

"Are you wearing fake eyelashes?" He leaned closer. "Is that *glitter*?"

"Oh, honey! Yes! Don't you *love* them?" She batted again and one of the eyelashes fell a bit sideways. Now it looked as if she had a glittery caterpillar flapping from her eyelid, but the old bird was carrying it off somehow.

Caught by the sudden thought that someday, and probably not that very many years from now, Maureen wouldn't be around to bother him, to ring his doorbell too early, to complain about his life choices, to make him drink tea that he hated, to bug him about taking his vitamins—Hank's heart constricted painfully. "Gramma." He held out his hand.

She immediately dropped the end of her knitting needle and tucked her hand in his.

It was colder than he would have thought. Dry, and small. The hand that had given him so much. "I love you, old woman. You know that, right?"

She squinted in suspicion and the eyelash flapped wildly. "Are you moving to Mexico?"

He gave a shout of laugher and released her hand. "Do you have my brain tapped? Is that it? I'm not going anywhere. Not without you, anyway."

"Good. Because if we go anywhere, I'd rather go somewhere I can speak the language. Boca Raton." She jabbed a stitch with her needle. "And she's not coming with us."

"Has anyone ever told you you're stubborn and closed-minded?"

She smiled beatifically. "*Thank* you. I love you, too, you big ridiculous child."

CHAPTER 14

T HREE WEEKS LATER, Samantha finally agreed to meet her sister for a juice.

A juice.

If you'd told Samantha when she was twenty-five that she'd ever make a date to meet Grace for a drink that didn't include alcohol, she would have fallen right off her barstool.

But Juice Blaster was the newest venture in town, and Grace had apparently already made best friends with the woman who owned it.

"Yay! You came!" Grace got off the seat that actually did resemble many a barstool Samantha had occupied during her drinking life. "I was worried you wouldn't be able to handle the fumes."

Samantha's nose twitched. "What *is* that?"

"Wheatgrass." Grace eyes were bright with excitement. "And guess what else? Roxie agreed to make a big batch of it for me every day in the morning, so my patients can have it before their acupuncture sessions. Here, I got you a shot, too."

The painful irony was that it *was* in a shot glass. Grace

hadn't held a shooter in a long, long time, but the weight of the glass felt just right in her hand. "One gulp?"

"I like to sip mine, but most people shoot it, yeah." Grace held up her own. "To your health."

Samantha drank the bright green liquid.

Then she was pretty sure she was going to die.

"Liquid health."

"No, that was the worst thing that was ever in my mouth, and once I woke up in an alley with my mouth lying in a puddle of something I couldn't identify."

Samantha had been mostly kidding—the puddle had been rainwater—but Grace suddenly looked like she was going to cry. "That's awful."

"Oh, honey, I was just teasing."

"No." Grace set her barely-tasted wheatgrass on the bar and sat back down on her stool. "That's where you where. In an alley. All those years when I couldn't find you—"

"Oh, sweetie...I always made it home for Christmas..."

"Except for that one year you didn't." Grace looked up at the menu board, blinking rapidly. "I'm glad you're home."

Samantha shook her head, but she got it. She did. "I'm glad I am, too." She leaned her shoulder against her sister's and looked up at the towering menu. "So what should I get?"

"The Green Giant is what I always get."

"Does that really say kale and beets?"

"It's delicious. Refreshing. She puts just a touch of fresh lemon, and you wouldn't believe—"

"Is there anything with ice cream?" Samantha asked with rising panic. She needed to get the wheatgrass taste out of her mouth, ASAP. Her teeth felt like they were wearing sweaters made of mud.

"Yes, but that's not why we're here."

Samantha smiled at Grace and said, "I'm here for sugar. If there's a sugar option, I'm taking it. You should know that by now."

"Fine. But get a booster, would you?"

Once they'd slid the straws into their huge drinks and opened the bag that held gluten-free chocolate-chip cookies, Samantha waited for Grace to ask.

"So," her sister said. "How's the apartment? Now that it's really cold, are those windows thick enough? Or are they letting in the draft like I thought they would? Because I've had this window guy coming in to see me, and he's super nice, and if you need to ask Johannes for better insulation, I'll help you do it."

Samantha stared at her. "You're not going to ask me about Hank?"

Grace gave her an innocent look. "What about him?"

"How the training is going?"

"Okay. How's it going?"

The training was amazing. Hank and she hadn't said a single word about the kiss in the car—they'd just worked. For three weeks now, Hank had been training with her every day he had off from the fire department. He was a natural. His physicality seemed to be an extension of his intelligence—she told him one thing, and he remembered it, incorporating what she said into the maneuver they were working on. After four sessions, she deemed him ready to shadow Wally Atkins, her other attacker, and in three of those training sessions, Hank was almost better than Wally was. He was quick, light on his feet, but he was absolutely committed to bringing his full body weight to bear when needed.

In their last session, Wally had to leave early, leaving Hank and Samantha to finish their work. Hank had taken her to the ground, almost pinning her. Samantha had been startled, then pleased he was doing so well. He was on top of her, and something had shifted. Something different and darker. Hotter. The feel of his body wasn't something she was fighting against, it was something she wanted. Again. For one heart-stopping moment, she laid under him and wondered what he would do if she took off his mask and arched up to kiss him.

Then she'd twisted her way out and had brought her foot down on top of his padded headgear in an attacker-stopping blow.

"It's great," she said to her sister.

"Is he going to be able to work with your next class?"

It started on Monday, her new group of eight women. "I think so. Wally can make most of the sessions, and Hank will be there for as many as he can, too, but there are a couple of times when it's just going to be Hank. I think he's going to do just fine."

"That's awesome." Her sister sucked up something just as green as the wheatgrass had been. "How's your smoothie?"

"I've never been so grateful for ice cream in my whole life." Why wasn't her sister digging for info on Hank? "I kissed him."

"I know," said Grace equanimously.

"Excuse me?"

"You know Darling Bay. If one person sees you necking in a Mustang, then it's common knowledge at Mabel's in the morning. I heard the next day."

"That was three *weeks* ago. You spent three weeks hiding this knowledge from me?"

"Me?" squeaked Grace. "You're the one who hid it! You didn't tell me, so I didn't ask. I figured if you wanted to give your old boyfriend a blast from the past, it was none of my business."

Samantha stared. "Who *are* you?"

Grace looked down. "I've been trying."

They'd gone rounds and rounds over the years. For long years, Grace had been the one to pick Samantha back up after the inevitable crash-landing, and she'd gotten in the habit. Samantha had made it crystal clear that she didn't need her older sister picking up after her any more. Her life was hers, to screw up or to fix, and she'd asked Grace to back off and let her fly with her own wings.

Grace had done a great job at letting go, and Samantha knew it hadn't been easy on her.

"I guess..." Samantha started.

Grace kept her eyes down, focused on the straw she was bending back and forth. "Yeah?"

"Maybe you could pry a little."

Exhaling loudly, Grace moved her smoothie and thumped her body forward onto the table. "Thank *goodness*. I've been *dying*. Do you know how much I've been dying over this? Not asking you? Are you *kidding* me? Oh, man. I did good. Give me a sip of that ice cream thingie."

Laughing, Samantha handed over her not-so-healthy smoothie.

"Ahhh. *Now tell me about the kiss.* Have there been more?"

Samantha shook her head. "Strictly business."

"Why?"

It felt good to trust her sister with this, to lean on her. "Maybe it was the emotional whiplash of firing and rehiring him in the space of seven seconds or something, but I needed him as an attacker."

"And you're scared it might be more than just business?"

Samantha scanned the very light freckles across Grace's nose, knowing she had the same kind across her own. "What if I don't...what if I can't stay?"

Her voice suddenly tight, Grace said, "When?"

"No, as far as I know, I'm not going anywhere. But..." The world was big. Samantha had seen so little of it. Her mother had seen even less.

"You don't want to hurt him again."

Samantha just nodded, feeling sick to her stomach.

"But you want to kiss him again."

Sighing, Samantha leaned on her elbows. "Have you *seen* him? Of course I do. And he's wonderful. The other day he brought me six extension cords."

"And that's...the wonderful part?"

"He noticed the extension cords in my apartment weren't surge protectors, so he brought me better ones."

Grace twisted in her chair.

"What?" Samantha knew her sister was trying not to say something.

"What would you have said if I'd given you six extension cords?"

Huh. If Grace had tried to upgrade something in her apartment, she would have accused her sister of meddling. "I would have called you bossy."

"So why don't you think that about him?"

"I do, a little. I was a tiny bit annoyed that he thought I wouldn't buy the cords for myself."

"But you hadn't."

Samantha said, "I concede that I hadn't. Don't ask if I've installed them yet because you don't want to know."

Grace shook her head, but her smile bordered on admiring. "You're the most stubborn person in the world."

"Not stubborn. More bull-headed. And not that much sense." Samantha sighed. "But I still want to kiss him, and I'm *really* trying to get over that."

"Or you could just go for it."

Surprised, Samantha said, "You're the one who's supposed to talk me out of it."

"Why?"

"Because he's bossy. He thinks he can fix people, and as you can attest, that's not my favorite trait in a person. Because he and I are oil and water. He's already figured out his dream, and he's living it, right here in the same small town he grew up in. I'm still chasing my dream, and I'm not going to stay here forever."

"Then have right now."

It was the last thing she expected to hear from her sister, the cautious one. "Are you serious?"

Grace nodded. "Grab right now. It's all we have. Don't worry about what's going to happen tomorrow."

"What if I hurt him?"

Tilting her head to the side, Grace said, "You know you're talking about a grown man, right?"

"But I hurt him once..."

"When he was a boy. You were both practically children. You were pretending to be grown up, that's what we all did at that age. I'm pretty darn sure Hank has made his own decisions for a long time now, and if it makes you feel better, then just be honest with him."

"And tell him what? That I'd like to kiss him—"

"That's all you want?"

"That's all I'm going to admit to my *sister*," said Samantha, kicking Grace's sneaker lightly with her own. "I should just kiss him and tell him that I'm going to leave at some point and that I can't be held liable for his heart?"

"Why not? It's honest."

"Should I get him to put it in writing? To get it notarized. To make it all legal?"

"How does he make you feel?"

Kissing him had felt like drinking a glass of wine and wanting the rest of the bottle. One gulp, and she'd wanted all of him. Maybe *that* was why it felt so dangerous. She'd had the one sip, and now he was all she could think about, day and night. "He makes me feel like I'm addicted to him or something. That's a bad thing in addict-world."

"Love is bad?"

"Well, no, it's a good thing, but...*what?* This isn't love. I can't believe you said that." What Samantha couldn't believe was that for one second, she'd gone along with the word without kneeing it and wrestling it to the ground.

Grace just smiled. "Keep me posted. I'm not going to ask. But tell me about it when you want to. Okay?"

"Jeez."

"What?"

"It's like you're my friend or something."

Grace grinned, and Samantha felt happiness flood her. "Sorry," said Grace. "Should I pinch you?"

"Yeah, that might help."

Her sister reached across the table and pinched her wrist.

"Ow." Samantha rubbed it. "That's better."

CHAPTER 15

THERE WERE EIGHT women in the new class, and Hank knew all but two of them. It was a small town—he shouldn't have been surprised that Dot Rilo from the post office had signed up with her best friend, Kayla. They never did anything without each other.

Gina and Tina and Kelly were there, too, which was a little more surprising. The three sisters were joint owners of the Wooden Duck, all in their early thirties. They'd inherited the bar from their dad, but all of them had worked there since they were of age to serve liquor. If anyone could handle themselves around ill-intentioned men, he would have thought it would have been them. Somehow, seeing them laughing together, their giggles sounding a little nervous, made the purpose of the class even more real.

Linda McCracken was there, too, and Hank was glad. He knew her from having responded to her house regularly when her husband was dying of prostate cancer. In the six months it had taken him to die, he'd gotten thinner and thinner, and Linda had wasted away along with him. It got to the point that when she would call 911 to get him back to the hospital, Hank would take a precious fifteen seconds to run to the kitchen to throw together whatever they'd eaten for dinner—pot roast piled on a plate with some leftover asparagus, or some chili tossed into a bowl—and while the medics packaged Len up, Hank would heat the food in her microwave while hiding her car keys. "No," he'd say. "No driving to the hospital until after you've eaten that." It got to the point where Linda didn't even try to talk him out of it. She'd sit obediently at the table, eating whatever it was with a blank expression. She moved slower every day. The afternoon the ambulance had taken Len away code three, the day Hank had known her husband wouldn't ever come back to the house, Hank didn't make her eat. They hadn't let her drive, either, taking her themselves. She'd finally cried that day. She'd cried the whole way.

He hadn't seen her in more than a year, probably. She smiled to see him, and hugged him. She'd lost even more weight. There was no way she could weigh more than ninety pounds, even with her big sneakers on.

The two women he didn't know—both of whom looked like soccer-moms—looked sideways at each other and carefully avoided eye contact with both him and Wally.

It felt weird to be instantly sized up as "a potential assailant," as Samantha had done when introducing them. Hank had been tall since his first real growth spurt at fourteen, but he'd never felt as hulking as he did now. He tried to school his features into a neutral blandness.

He tried to think about kittens and puppies. Puffy puffs of...soft puffiness.

And even still, Hank felt menacing in his skin.

Samantha was good at her job. After the first couple of minutes, during which she took them all on a little tour of her "gym," the corner of the community center where she'd dragged out the large blue mats, she directed everyone to sit in a small circle in the middle of the mat. Relieved, Hank sat next to Wally, and they both hunched forward. Linda sat on his left, and he noticed that her hands were shaking slightly in her lap. He wanted so badly to lean over and put his arm around her shoulders for a quick squeeze, the way he had many times before, but the tension she radiated was crystalline, and he was afraid he might break her. He settled on resolving to make the slowest movements possible while he was near her.

How that would work when he was pinning her down, he had no idea. Use all his strength on Linda? No way. He wouldn't be able to do that. Hank was sure that when he and Wally met with Samantha afterward, she'd agree with his assessment.

Samantha explained what the women would learn in the three-day course, using language that was clear and encouraging. She took the helmet of one of the men's body suits and put it on her own head. The women laughed, but the free-floating tension had coalesced, and now hovered thickly in the circle.

Hank tried harder to think of puppies and cotton balls.

Samantha took off the helmet and passed it around, saying, "Look. Feel this. See how thick this is? There's no blow that you can land to this that will damage the person inside it. In this class, you'll learn to use your powerful words and voice. Also, your body will learn how to hit the person wearing that helmet so hard that in real life, if he wasn't wearing a body suit, he'd be stopped and you'd be safe."

Hank felt the tremor in Linda's hands as she passed him the helmet. He tried to catch Samantha's eye. Linda wasn't ready for this. Maybe it wasn't such a great idea for her to be here.

But if Samantha noticed Linda's nerves, she didn't let on.

"Some of you may be wondering if you're up for this."

Gina elbowed Kelly in the ribs with a grin.

"But I have to tell you, we all think that when we start learning this stuff. Some parts of this class might be scary, and some might be painful, but I'm pretty sure you're going to be surprised to learn how much *fun* this is going to be, too. Now." Samantha smiled at the sisters, and something deep inside Hank twisted. "Now, I'm going to tell you why I do this. Then we're going to go around the circle and tell each other why we're here."

Linda gave an almost silent moan, just under her breath.

Samantha went on, "Your reason for being here might be awful. Your reason might be the most painful thing you ever went through. Whatever that reason is, it's safe to share here. If you can't, I understand. I really do. But I'd encourage you to share as much as you feel you can. Nothing will leave this room. Okay, me first." Samantha glanced at Hank, and for the first time, he could see that she was nervous, too. No one else in the room could tell, he would be willing to bet. But there it was, that tiny little catch in her breath that sometimes happened between her words.

Samantha twisted her fingers together. "What happened to me was a long time ago, and sometimes it feels as fresh as if it happened yesterday. I..." She cleared her throat. "I was working at a pizza joint in Reno, and I was closing. The night manager and I were friends, and we'd had a couple of beers each. He was doing the money, I was mopping. When we were done with the duties, we went outside for a smoke."

Hank hadn't ever considered the idea that maybe *she* had a good reason for teaching this class.

He was a freaking idiot.

"Then he asked me if I wanted to have sex with him. When I said no, he informed me that in fact, I did. He forced me, physically, behind the dumpster where we stored the extra fryer oil, and he raped me."

Hank's hands were clenched into fists. He rubbed them against his thighs, but it didn't help. How could something like that have happened to her? Hank wanted to find out the guy's name, find him on Facebook and track him down. Then he wanted to pull him out of his house and push him behind a dumpster and have his own way with him, a way that would have nothing to do with sex and everything to do with knuckles smashing the guy's face in.

"Then he offered me a raise. I said that I quit. And he laughed." Her voice did that little catch thing again on the last word. "That was maybe the worst part. That he laughed at me while I was driving off. For months—no, years—I imagined other ways that could have gone down. I could have learned how to fight, and I could have gone back and beaten him up. I could have found someone to do it for me."

Hank barely kept himself from shouting that he volunteered. At the same time, he wanted to apologize for his entire gender and slink away, out of the community center, and hide somewhere dark and deep so that he wouldn't accidentally scare a woman anywhere, ever.

"I thought of a million different things I wanted to say to him, and none of them were exactly right. I spent *years* thinking about him. Then I took a class much like this one, and I finally learned what I needed to know how to say. I learned how to say *NO*, how to keep saying it, how to yell and scream and rage and fight and punch and kick. I finally learned that no one could take care of me better than I could of myself. That was when I finally started sleeping through the night." Her voice was soft now, and encouraging. "Okay. Going around to my right, how about you, Gina? Tell us why you're here and what you hope to learn."

Gina said in a tight voice that she was there for her sister Kelly. Tina said the same thing. Then Kelly, with a sister hanging on to each hand, said in a voice that was strangely strong for the words they carried, "I was raped at knifepoint in the women's bathroom of our bar last year. What I hope to learn from this class is how to get over that."

Not how to cut the son of a bitch who might try to touch her in the future. Not how to beat someone up, not how to protect someone else. Kelly wanted to know how to get *over* it. The horror Hank felt was deep and sickening.

Samantha nodded. "No one gets over all of it, that's the sad part. The really good part, though, is that with the right tools, we can move *past* it, into a better, stronger place. You're going to love this, Kelly. I can't wait for you to learn these tools." Samantha's voice was warm, and some of the tension in Kelly's face relaxed.

This was what Samantha was meant to do. This was her passion, her reason, her thing. And damn, there was nothing as sexy in the whole world as watching the woman you loved do exactly what she was best at.

Oh, man.

Hank loved her.

Okay, yeah, he'd had maybe a hint that it was coming—his history with her, instead of inoculating him, had made him perhaps a little more susceptible, he'd known that. But he thought he would have had a little more time to fight it off.

Hank hadn't fought it off, not at all. And the realization made him feel like he was invincible, even though the opposite had just been proven. Samantha met his eyes and though her face showed nothing but attentive concern to the women she was working with, something behind her gaze warmed as their eyes locked.

Something for him.

Pull it together, Coffee. There was only one thing that was important in this moment, and it was listening to the next woman talking. But something remained inside his chest, a warmth that was intoxicating, like whiskey poured straight into his veins.

Linda McCracken was still tucked into herself next to him, her legs pulled up to her chest. Samantha's voice was soft. "Your turn, Linda. Can you tell us why you're here?"

She shook her pale head and put her chin on her knees. "I don't think so," she said in a small voice.

"Are you sure? I'm totally willing to go to the next person, but something tells me that you need to say something." Samantha scooted forward so that she was sitting right in front of Linda, a foot away. In a low voice, meant just for Linda, she said, "You can whisper it to me if you want. Then I can tell the class, or we can keep it just between us, whichever you'd like."

There was a pause during which it felt like the whole class was holding its collective breath. Hank knew he was.

Then Linda nodded. Samantha leaned forward and Linda put her lips next to Samantha's ear. Hank was closer than anyone else, but Linda kept her whisper so low he didn't catch a single word.

Samantha gave Linda a brief, fierce hug. She scooted

back to her place and said without preamble, "Linda would like you to know that she was raped when she was young. Her husband made her feel safe. Now that he's gone, she's back to being scared in her home." Samantha looked directly at Linda. "After this class, you won't be scared anymore. I try not to promise things, but I'm going to promise you this. You will not be scared, and I'm going to see to that."

Linda made a whuffling sound and put her forehead back on her knees.

Hank desperately wanted to *do* something. That was how he'd been trained, how he lived his life. You helped, you ran toward the problem, you worked until it was fixed. You protected.

But Samantha caught his gaze, and as if reading his thoughts, gave the smallest shake of her head.

She was right. Linda gave off fear in huge, brittle waves. If Samantha could pull off helping this woman, Hank would have to marry her.

If she'd have him.

Hank's heart was lost and might end up crushed, and he suspected his ass was about to be kicked in their demo for the women.

And he'd never been happier in his life.

CHAPTER 16

S AMANTHA PULLED UP in front of Hank's house. If he hadn't said the other night that he lived on Lowry, she wouldn't have even known where to look for his Mustang. It felt...a little stalkerish, maybe, to be driving up and down a street in the dark, looking under the streetlights for a man's car.

It didn't make sense. None of it did. It probably wasn't the right thing to do. Samantha should go to Grace's house. Grace would take care of her. She had some hippie echinacea-mint tea that made you relax and feel alert all at the same time. Samantha had bought the tea herself, but somehow, making it for herself at the apartment didn't feel the same. Sure, it was nice taking it out on the balcony and watching the boats chug in and out of the marina, offloading things like crabs, loading up tourists and heading back out again, the mug of tea warm in her hands. But at Grace's house, her sister took care of everything. She made Samantha sit in that perfectly soft chair in the kitchen where it was always warm and smelled of ginger.

That's what she should do. She would show up, and like

always, Grace would take care of her. It would feel good to be coddled, and then she'd go home and sleep like the dead.

Instead, she was here. Searching for a guy who probably didn't even want her to find him. Before she'd come back to town, if she'd been asked, she would have said that she remembered Hank Coffee as a sweet man. Smart. Funny.

That was before she'd learned that he was also the three things she always fell for—good looking, dangerous, and sexy as hell.

Which was why it was a very bad idea to be walking up the path in the dark to his front door.

A low-slung green house, it was a fifties ranch style, the kind of house Samantha and Grace had always wanted to live in when they were kids. The kind of house where the garage was built to be full of bicycles and cardboard boxes holding old crafts: God's eyes made of yarn and chopsticks, and snowmen made from cardboard and cotton balls. The light on the porch burned brightly, welcoming. The door-bell was loud inside. She heard laughter and a woman's voice from behind the door.

Whoa. What if he *did* have a girlfriend and no one talked about her? What if they had an agreement, and Hank was welcome to make out with other girls in his car, just as long as he didn't sleep with them? What if that was the real reason why he left the other night? What if a pretty, petite, well-mannered woman opened the door? What was Saman-tha's excuse going to be?

Training! Sure. They had a few more moves to go over before the next class. That was it.

The door was opened by a woman, all right, but she most likely wasn't girlfriend material. Eighty-five if she was a day, Samantha knew her as one of the women who knitted in the back booths at Mabel's Cafe. She was wearing a lemon-yellow sweater with an embroidered blue rocket on the front, and her gray hair was flying out of its bun.

"Hi, I'm Samantha Rowe."

"I know," the woman said.

Then, without another word, she shut the door in Samantha's face.

Oh. Well, that was one answer to the question of whether this was a good idea or not. Samantha turned to leave, but her steps faltered when her foot was on the second step.

She turned back around.

This time she knocked instead of ringing the bell.

The door jerked open. "Yes?"

"Is Hank home?"

"Yes." The older woman started to close the door again, but Samantha wedged her boot in the crack.

"Good," said Samantha. "Can you tell him I'm here?"

"No."

Really? That's what she got for screwing up her courage to find him? She probably deserved a lot, but as far as she knew, she didn't deserve this. "Good grief, lady, what did I do to you?"

The door opened a few inches wider but Samantha didn't pull her foot back. If she had, she knew the door would have been shut and locked again in a heartbeat.

"You didn't do anything to me," said the woman.

"I didn't think so."

"You hurt my grandson. A long time ago." The woman scowled. Her eyelashes looked crooked and sparkly. "But I'm still mad at you for it."

That was totally fair. "Yeah, well, me too."

A surprised look played across the woman's face. "You're mad at yourself?"

"Completely. I was a stupid kid who didn't know a good thing when I saw it."

The door opened another eight inches. "You're right. You didn't. He's the best boy in the world."

Samantha wrinkled her nose. "I wouldn't call him a boy anymore. Would you?"

The woman clutched the door jam. "Of course. He'll always be my boy. You can't blame me for trying to protect him."

Hank's voice rose from somewhere inside. "Gramma? Who is it?"

"No one," said the woman over her shoulder, but then she appeared to relent. "Just that girl who smashed your heart into tiny little pieces when you were twenty-one."

"*Samantha?*"

Hank came into the hallway, and Samantha lost her breath. He was barefoot, wearing a white tank top that showed off every one of the sizable muscles in his upper torso and bulging arms. Faded black sweat pants hung from his hips. He was carrying a plate that looked like it had held pasta of some kind. A strand of too-long dark hair dropped over his eye, and Samantha wanted to rush him and kiss, grandmother notwithstanding.

And the way his eyes had heated to see her, she was pretty sure he might allow her to.

"Gramma, let her in."

"Over my dead body." But the words weren't said as roughly as they could have been, and it was the woman who pulled the door all the way open, not Hank. "Just for a minute. But then you have to go, girl."

"My house, my rules, Grams." Hank bent to kiss his grandmother's cheek, and Samantha's heart grew two sizes.

"Samantha, this is Maureen, my pistol-packin' grandmother. Maureen, this is Samantha."

Maureen trundled ahead through the hallway, grumbling something about pasta sauce and a waste of meat. Hank and Samantha let her go into the next room.

Samantha's newly huge heart pounded heavily.

Hank leaned against the wall, appearing comfortable in his own skin.

His eyes smoldered darkly. "What's up, trouble?"

"I thought..." What had she thought again?

"Yeah?" His voice was a purr. Damn him.

"About class. A thing. I, um, just wanted to go over a couple of things."

"Uh-huh." He wasn't buying it, she could tell.

"But I can just catch you up later. At the next class."

"Okay."

From around the corner came Maureen's voice. "Are you two coming into the kitchen, or should I just go home by myself in the dark?"

Never taking his eyes off hers, Hank stepped forward. He got so close to Samantha that her breathing hitched in her chest, and she could feel the heat coming from his body. He lifted her hair from where it lay on her shoulder and put his mouth on her neck, just below her ear. It was the softest touch, the lightest caress of his lips, and it made Samantha's legs tremble. He brought his mouth up slowly, so slowly, up the curve of her jaw, pressed a final kiss against the top of her cheekbone, right next to her temple. She could hear him breathing next to her, and his breath was as ragged as hers.

He dropped her hair back to her shoulder and stepped back.

"Coming," Hank called, never taking his eyes off hers. His gaze heated to the point where Samantha thought she might melt into a puddle on the spot. His eyes promised something that, heaven help her, she was going to stick around to take. Hank was heated steel tension, his body taut, rigid with need.

If his grandmother wasn't in the next room, Samantha would have walked right past Hank, shedding clothes as she went, hoping to find the bedroom, and not caring if she didn't find it. The living room would be just fine. The kitchen. The laundry room would have been hot at this point.

How had she *not* slept with him back then? Had he looked at her this way? There was no way he'd had that heavy-lidded gaze back then. He'd been just a kid, and so had she.

But the Hank Coffee who stood in front of her now was raw need, barely controlled lust. A muscle in his jaw tightened. He was all man. One hundred and twenty masculine percent.

"Excuse me? Can you hear me or not?"

"Sorry," he grated. "She's not going to stop calling us."

"Didn't figure she would. I'll just see you later, okay? She doesn't want me in there."

"Maybe not. But I do."

CHAPTER 17

T HE KITCHEN WAS all male, dark green walls with deep blue accents. It also looked like a kitchen that was used. The two pots sitting on top of the stove looked well-loved, burnished with age and scrubbing. There was a clock made out of a record above the stove. Samantha tiptoed to read the disc label.

"Prince's Purple Rain," Hank said. "And I make no apology for it."

"Nor should you," said Samantha in admiration.

"He's stuck in the 80s," said Maureen, her back to them as she scrubbed a plate.

"She's stuck in the 90s," said Hank easily. He moved in next to Maureen, dropping his plate in the soapy water. He looked at Samantha. "Have you eaten?"

"Oh, I'm fine," said Samantha. Her stomach took that moment to grumble loudly. She put her hand over her belly. "Whoops."

"You like mostaccioli? Gramma makes the best."

"We're out," grumped Maureen. "All out."

"Bull." Hank pulled out a foil-covered glass pan from

the fridge. "Still warm. Grab me a plate from that cabinet." He gestured with his chin.

Samantha complied, wondering how handy Maureen was with her needles. Was she going to stab her with them? Or was she handier with a knife? Samantha resolved to keep all her extremities to herself.

Hank dished out a huge portion.

"I can't eat all that."

"We're carbo-loading for class," he said.

"I teach. I stand there and yell. You're the one who might want to eat a few more calories. Those women aren't joking around."

Hank caught her gaze again, sending her that look, the one that sent a shiver of lust through her body right down to her very toes. When he handed her the full plate, she caught his scent—he smelled faintly of wood shavings and pine, as if he'd been sharpening pencils in the woods. It was both a comforting and heady scent.

"Sit," he said. "Eat."

It was easier to just comply.

Maureen, her hands dripping with soapy water, turned and fixed Samantha with a stare. Her fork stilled in mid-air.

"You still drinking?"

It felt like a slap. But it was a fair question. It just hurt that the recovery she'd prefer to keep hidden was common knowledge for the whole town. She knew how gossip worked. She was—dimly—aware of the way she'd acted in the Wooden Duck on the few occasions she'd come back to town before getting sober. One Christmas Eve, she'd walked to the bar and she hadn't made it back to Grace's until the day after Christmas. The actual holiday itself was lost to her —she'd met a guy during her blackout and if she'd woken up to find out they'd gotten married, she wouldn't have been surprised. The feeling of embarrassment was still so painful that she could almost not bear to think of it. But that was part of how she managed to stay sober. That pain.

"No, ma'am."

"Will you start again?"

"I hope not."

"Can you promise you won't?"

Wouldn't that be nice? Samantha would love to be positive she wouldn't ever take another drink. She was pretty sure she wouldn't. But she knew that the one thing she had to do was look at one day. Today. "I can promise I won't today."

"Do you think that's good enough?" Maureen folded a red dish towel over her arm.

"It's the best I can do."

"Humph." But Maureen's voice had softened a bit. "I guess you're trying."

"I am." Samantha decided she'd take a risk and take a bite of the woman's food. The knitting needles were still in their basket and the worst that Maureen might do right now was snap her with the wet towel. A forkful of the mostaccioli proved to be as delicious as it had smelled. "This is wonderful."

Maureen didn't answer but took a plastic-wrapped block of parmesan out of the refrigerator and grated some over the top of the plate. "Needs more cheese."

"Thank you."

Maureen said, "I'm leaving you the dishes, Hank. Come see me tomorrow." She straightened her sweater which was wet at the belly button area.

"I thought you were going to make me watch that dancing show you like."

Raising an eyebrow at Samantha, Maureen said, "I

think you're busy tonight. I can't say I approve of you, girl. You know he hasn't fallen in love since you? I blame you for that. For scaring him."

That couldn't be true. Samantha tried to catch Hank's eye but he busied himself drying a fork meticulously. "How is that possible? Hank?"

"Come on, Gramma, you know I'm not scared of anything but a scolding from you. Love just isn't for me. I fall in deep like as often as I can, though." He gave Samantha a cheeky grin and tossed the fork in a drawer with a flourish.

Maureen wasn't done. "How do I know you won't hurt him all over again?"

"It's just like the drinking," said Samantha. "I can only try not to do that again today."

Maureen picked up her knitting basket and held it to her chest. "Try hard. As hard as you can." She went up on tiptoe to kiss Hank's cheek goodbye. "You be good, too. Don't either of you let me down."

She slammed the door on her way out.

Hank laughed. "That was her last word. I'm sorry about that."

Samantha spoke around another mouthful. "This pasta would be worth her giving me a sharp punch to the nose."

"It's my favorite. You picked a good night to come by. To train, I mean."

But there it was, in his eyes again. That banked, quiet heat, the look that seemed to say so much more. Samantha's appetite suddenly fled. "Train," she repeated weakly. Like the one that was about to hit her.

"That's what you said you came by for, right?"

"Um. Yeah." That's what she'd said. What she'd *meant* to do was kiss him. She'd meant to march in, wrap her arms around his neck and not stop kissing him until he ran out of protests and took her to his bed. They'd work out what to do the next day. Samantha knew that leaping before you looked might not be the best game plan in all cases, but in sex? Sometimes you just get something out of your system. Maybe it would help her get over these jangling nerves she felt whenever he was near, the sense that nothing else mattered but touching him, getting her skin next to his.

Hank angled his head like his neck hurt. "Or we could just go to bed."

Samantha's mouth fell open and she forgot how to speak, which was fine, since she wouldn't have known what to say, anyway. She'd planned to make it happen, not to talk about. And that was before she'd been derailed by an angry grandmother.

"You know. Get it out of the way."

"Yes!" Samantha felt light with relief. "That's it!"

"Way I figure it, we've had it building up between us for what, thirteen years? Might be time to just jump right in the sack."

Samantha coughed and took a sip of the water he'd given her.

"Naked, I mean," Hank clarified. "In case you didn't think that's what I meant."

"Mmm. I..."

"You want to go there now?"

"To bed," she hedged.

"My bed."

"With you," said Samantha.

"All six foot three of me. If you don't mind a—" he paused for effect "—big guy."

Samantha wondered if it was actually possible to faint

from lust. "I'm not sure talking about it so...prosaically is exactly the way it usually goes."

"What?" Hank said, hooking a leg around the chair next to her and pulling it toward him. He straddled it like a horse, looking long and easy in his body. "This kind of planning? I reckon that sometimes thinking about something you want is almost as fun as getting it. And I've got to tell you, I've sure spent some quality time thinking about the way you're going look under me."

"Oh!"

"I like thinking about the way you'll feel against my body, when I'm moving against you. I like wondering how your breasts will fit in my hands." Hank held out his fingers and looked at them, and Samantha noticed again how very large his hands were. "I like thinking about how soft you'll feel and I like wondering how wet I can make you before you come."

"Oh," she said again. There weren't any other words left in the world.

"I like thinking about that last moment, right before you climb to the top, when I'm inside you. Your hair is all over my pillow, and your eyes are closed and then you cry out and you look at me, and then I kiss you. Hard."

Samantha touched her lips. She could almost feel it, could almost feel him holding himself over her.

"What do we do now?" she whispered.

He rocked forward on the chair so that they were only inches apart. "We go in my bedroom. I take off your clothes. You take off mine. Then we get in the bed."

"Naked."

"Extremely naked."

She stood, unsure if her knees would hold her up.

"Don't you worry," he said. "I'll catch you if you fall."

CHAPTER 18

H ANK WOKE UP with Samantha in his arms. She was cradled perfectly against his chest, her cheek on his shoulder as if she'd slept there for years. She breathed steadily, a dark strand of hair fluttering in front of her mouth every time she exhaled. Samantha Rowe was not only the sexiest woman he'd ever seen, she was also the cutest.

His plan had failed spectacularly.

When he'd seen her standing on the other side of Maureen in his doorway, with that look on her face, the look she couldn't hide from him even though she tried to be all business in front of his grandmother, he'd decided he'd go along with her.

He'd get her out of his system. He'd give just about anything not to feel this way about her. *In love.*

Honestly, last night Hank had hoped that one good roll in the hay would clear his brain, for once and for all.

Instead, he woke up and realized that he still wasn't over her. Maybe he never would be.

And that just sucked, because if he knew one thing

about Samantha Rowe, it was that she wasn't a good bet. Above anything else, Hank used to want safety. Now he wanted Samantha. How the hell was that safe?

And while maybe he should be upset about it, he wasn't.

Instead, even though his plan had backfired, Hank realized he was in just about the best mood of his life. Right there, in that pile of sunlight and sheets, with Samantha lying on his shoulder.

She stirred, stretching her legs and giving a slight, low groan in the back of her throat. Hank felt himself get hard again.

Nuzzling herself under his chin, Samantha pressed her nose against the stubble of his jaw and made another throaty noise.

Then he felt her jerk backward. She gasped.

In an instant, she was sitting upright, the sheet pulled up to her chin. "Oh, *man*." She rubbed her eyes with her free hand. "I was just having this dream, and…"

He filled in the blank. "And then it wasn't a dream."

"Something like that."

"I'm going to make you some coffee. Don't leave."

She made a high-pitched noise and pulled the sheet over her head.

Hank laughed his way into the kitchen.

SHE HAD to get out of there. As fast as possible.

She'd done the worst thing she could have.

The worst thing *ever*.

And it wasn't sleeping with Hank Coffee.

That was the thing—sleeping with Hank had been

wonderful. Okay, there had been precious little sleeping involved, mostly there had been his fingers and his tongue and his glorious body...

He'd fit her like no man ever had. She'd felt beautiful in his arms, like a sexy tramp. Like a goddess.

But what had broken her, really, what had made it clear to her that this wasn't normal, none of it was, was when he'd kissed her at dawn. It had been a different kiss than all the others.

It was a kiss with a promise of the future.

Samantha didn't do the future. One day at a time wasn't a slogan to her, it wasn't just a motto. It was her life. Tomorrow, she might be gone. She could only bank on today. The only time she thought about the future was when she was planning her training class. When it came to the women she was responsible for, yes, she'd look into the future. But apart from that? She'd made sure to sign a month-to-month lease on her apartment, so she could leave at a moment's notice. She always bought a pint of half-and-half for her coffee, never a quart. Just in case.

Coffee. Hank Coffee was making her coffee.

And heaven help her, she was wishing he'd do that every day for the rest of her life.

Why did the word *love* keep sounding in her head like a bell she couldn't stop hearing? It was a quiet bell, as if she was hearing it from far away, but it was insistent and clear and beautiful.

Samantha groaned and covered her head with the pillow next to her. That only made it worse, though. It was *his* pillow and smelled deliciously of him—wood chips and pine and soap. She threw it to the foot of the bed and sat straight up, keeping the sheet over her naked breasts in case Hank walked in.

And what if he did? He'd pretty much seen all there was to see last night.

"Here you go, trouble." Hank was only wearing red checked boxers. His chest was so broad, so well-defined, the muscles that she'd traced last night with her lips disappearing into the top of his shorts...

It was light with cream, just the way she liked it. How did he know that about her?

He must have read her quizzical look. "You liked cream in college. I thought maybe you still did."

She nodded quickly and took a too-hot sip of the coffee. "Thanks. I've always liked it hot."

In response, he quirked an eyebrow.

Hot Coffee.

She laughed. "Oh, come on."

"I didn't say anything."

"Well, thank you."

In response, he dropped a kiss on her collarbone and moved to sit with his back against the headboard. "Anytime."

"You don't have to work today?" Part of her—okay, a big part—had been hoping he'd slide out of bed and go to work and she could start piecing together this new life, the one she couldn't make heads or tails of yet.

"Nope."

"I can't keep track of your schedule."

"Two days on, four days off."

"That's a lot of time off," she said weakly.

"More time with you."

Samantha's sip of coffee choked her as it went down the wrong way.

"Need help?"

She shook her head.

"Am I scaring you? With this together talk?"

"Are you always this blunt?" Like last night, when he hadn't so much talked her into bed as talked her straight at it.

"Only when I really want something."

Her. He wanted *her*.

Samantha didn't get it.

Hank was the total package, from his sexy surfer-boy hair to the fact that he *literally* helped little old ladies across the street (she'd seen him do it once after a training session). His job was saving *lives*. He ran into burning buildings instead of away.

Samantha didn't drink anymore. That was her claim to any kind of success. That and Daring Darling, which, yes, was her baby, and she prayed it grew into something really fine, something to be proud of.

But Hank was *Hank*. The boy she'd let go, the man she knew she'd never deserve, and instead, he was sitting on the bed with her, watching her as if he wanted more than just to kiss her. Watching her with such...generous, inviting warmth.

Maybe she *had* found something too terrifying. Maybe he was the cliff she wouldn't be brave enough to leap from.

Maybe safety was the thing she was most scared of.

"I should go," she said, splashing coffee on the bedding as she moved too quickly.

"What's the hurry?" He glanced at the clock. "You're not working at the bagel shop today or you would have been there two hours ago."

Good grief. She didn't work today, but that was only luck. When she'd fallen asleep in Hank's arms, she hadn't given a single thought to the next day. "I just have some things I have to do..."

"Okay. Wanna get breakfast first?"

She did. Oh, how she did. She wanted to borrow a fire department sweatshirt from him and go to Mabel's Cafe. She wanted to slide into a red booth across from him. She wanted to sneak bacon off his plate and laugh as regulars came up and talked to him just because he was Hank Coffee and everyone in town loved him.

If only she could do it. If only the security he offered didn't scare the hell out of her.

"I've got eggs at home. I've got to work on a fiscal report thing for the bank—they're just about ready to put the loan into my name..." Samantha caught her breath. Once her business was in her name and not her sister's, it made it real.

It meant she would stay. That she'd have no option of running. Not that she wanted to—she didn't. But she couldn't know she wouldn't want to someday. That wasn't fair to anyone, not to Grace, not to the man looking at her with such sweet intensity.

"Anyway," she went on lamely. "Thanks for the... I'll see you at the..."

"Samantha. I'm in love with you."

"Whoa, buddy. Back that truck up." She held up her hand as she clutched the sheet to her chest more tightly. "Um."

He laughed, and the world tilted on its axis. The only thing she wanted was to crawl into his lap and stay there forever. Instead, she scanned the room for her clothing. There, over the low chest of drawers, was her bra. Her shirt was on the floor by the closet, and who knew where her jeans had landed?

Hank leaned forward and cupped her face with one hand. "I'm so in love with you it hurts."

CHAPTER 19

S AMANTHA STUTTERED AS she spoke. "N-no, you're just... You're just feeling something from the past. You never recovered from the girl I was, and I'm sorry about that..."

"I never recovered from *you*. The woman you were and the woman you are, Sam. I'm in love with you and I figure I'll just keep telling you that. It's okay if you don't believe me today. But it's the truth. I think it's always been true. I just didn't know it until now." He whispered a kiss against her ear, sending chills down Samantha's back.

No, no. She couldn't do this to him. She scooted to the edge of the bed, taking the sheet with her. Swinging her legs to the floor, she said, "It won't last. I'm not a good bet." Man, that hurt to say out loud.

"I know you're not. But even so, I find myself wanting to risk it all on the dice."

"Yeah, well, I don't date gamblers."

"Maybe I'm just hoping I'm the lucky type."

Samantha couldn't help smiling. "Well, someone's glib

this morning. Are you always this silver-tongued when you wake up?"

"Only when my tongue's been recently limbered up."

Samantha felt herself blush.

Then she pressed the flat of her palm onto his chest. His skin was warm, the muscles taut. Oh, how she wanted to move her hand against him more, to feel... "Hank. Keep your heart safe for someone who deserves it."

He caught her hand and pressed it against his skin. "What about your heart?"

"It's good. Not broken." *Yet.* "Look, I'm just trying to keep us both safe."

He laughed and she felt the sound beat inside him. "That's my job."

"No."

"Oh, yeah." Hank leaned forward and pressed a quick kiss against her lips, surprising in its sweetness. How did he taste like that? Like everything Samantha had never known she wanted?

"I love you," he said. "I'll keep you safe. That's what I *want* to do."

The sadness felt like ice water. "But I don't need you to."

"You do," he said. "You've been hurt in the past. You deserve someone to take care of you."

"Sure, my heart's been broken—but I lived through it." Nothing she'd ever gone through would hurt like walking out Hank's door this morning was going to.

"But..." Hank paused and threaded his fingers with hers. "The rape. I know you don't..."

Samantha didn't talk about that. "Oh, no."

"I get it. I want you to know I'm here for you." It seemed like his chest broadened as he said the words, as if he thought he could physically shield her from everything that could hurt her.

But he did *not* get to bring that topic up to use it for his own gain. "I told the women that. Not you."

"You should have told me, though."

Samantha felt her heart speed up, pumping with sudden anger. She jerked her hand back. "No. I didn't have to do a thing. That's *my* history. Not yours."

"I want it to be ours." His voice softened. "You should have told me. I wish you had. I wish I could have been there for you, instead of hearing about it for the first time in front of strangers."

"But you couldn't help me." The rape had been one of the most terrible things that Samantha had ever experienced. It had also been *her* thing. She'd gotten through it. Maybe she hadn't handled it in the most healthy way possible, but that was because she hadn't known then what she knew now—that things didn't stay buried. That it was better to deal with things head-on before they roiled out of control. That alcohol and pills didn't help. That men who loved her, as earnest as they were, didn't help, either.

Which was exactly why she had to get out of here, before she broke her own heart, and so much worse, his. "Seriously, you couldn't have helped me back then. I wasn't very helpable."

Hank made a frustrated noise and reached over the edge of the bed to the floor. He jerked a blue fire department T-shirt over his head. "You don't know that. I want you to feel safe, the way Linda said she did when her husband was alive."

That was the whole problem. Linda needed to feel safe by *herself*. "Linda lost the one person she could rely on. That was a bet she lost. We all lose. You should understand risk better than anyone. You're a firefighter. You can't promise to come home to me." Not that she meant... "To anyone," she corrected herself.

Hank tilted his head. "There's risk, yeah. But I'm the safest one on the crew. I never leap before I look. Protocol is there for a reason, and I follow it—"

"Rules aren't all they're cracked up to be," Samantha said as gently as she could. "You're *too* safe. Remember, way back then, when you made me promise you that at least when I was with Vicente that I would always wear a helmet?"

"Yeah," he said. "Then you rode off into the sunset without one. I watched you go. I was so *mad* at you for that, Samantha."

"But I didn't die." She tugged on the sheet he'd pulled from her when he'd reached for his shirt.

"You could have."

"Gah! That's the point, Hank. I *didn't* die. It sounds obvious, but it's pretty simple: we don't die from the things that don't kill us. And the exhilaration we feel from doing the wrong thing can be amazing." Riding across the Mohave at a hundred miles an hour, the hot wind tearing at her hair —it had been one of the most stupid things she'd ever done, probably. She'd also never forget—or regret—that ride.

Hank shoved a hand through his messy hair. She'd given him that bedhead, she suddenly realized. Her fingers had done that to his hair last night. And again early that morning.

"No, we don't," he said, "but people die from the stupid, preventable things. An epileptic man forgot to take his medicine and fell into his fireplace last year."

Samantha gasped.

He went on. "What were the odds of that happening? A

billion to one? But he could have just chosen to wait to light the fire until his wife got home. That would have saved his life. A woman just last week died of asthma because she'd forgotten her inhaler while she was at the gym. Instead of asking them to call 911, she went to the locker room to catch her breath, and instead, died by herself. Stupid, preventable things."

Samantha flexed her fingers in the air as if trying to grasp what she needed. The right words were there, the ones that would make him understand this—she just had to find them. "Then *why* do you try to prevent things? You're just proving my point. You might as well do whatever you want. You're going to die anyway."

"Kids die, too. The ones whose parents didn't put them in the carseat, because they were only going around the block to grandma's house. A mother of ten-year-old twin girls was killed on her bicycle last year because she fell and hit her head. She wasn't wearing a helmet. She also wasn't carrying any ID, so for about eight hours, no one knew who she was. She was a Jane Doe at the hospital morgue."

Samantha shook her head, not wanting to hear any more, but he kept talking.

"I just kept thinking about her daughters and her husband, how long they waited for her to come home before calling the cops to report her missing. The sergeant on the call said they gave up waiting for her for dinner and went to get burgers, but none of them ate anything because they were so scared about her not coming home for the first time ever. How do you plan for that? You don't. But you know how you prevent it from happening? You take all the precautions you can. Like wearing your damn helmet which would have saved that woman's twins from growing up without a mother."

"Have you ever jumped out of a plane?"

He shook his head firmly. "No. I never would."

"Tempting fate?"

"Damn straight."

"So you'll never get to know that rush you feel as you fall and fall and then suddenly you've fallen past the place where you would normally stop and your body tells you you're going to die, and then you pull the ripcord, and you're safe, hanging under the parachute, and the next few minutes of drifting toward mother earth are the sweetest moments of your life." *Except for the moments after making love with the man with the eyes to match his last name.*

"You're not as daring as you think you are, you know."

Oh, if he was looking for a fight? This was the way to have it. Samantha dropped the sheet and slid off the edge of the bed. She glared at him, hands on her hips, too angry to be embarrassed to be naked in front of him. "Where are my jeans?"

"You're scared to lose your heart."

"I'm serious, Hank." She pulled her shirt over her head, not bothering with her bra. She'd shove that in her bag. "My jeans?"

"You're terrified to love. You're reckless—sometimes idiotically so—but you won't take a chance on love. Why is that?"

Her teeth started to chatter though she wasn't cold. "I. Need. My. Jeans."

"It's not the rape—rape is about power. It has to have been before that. Your dad?"

"Are you seriously going to analyze me? Can I put my pants on?"

He shrugged. "Check under the bed. Were your parents happy?"

Samantha scowled. "Very."

"Is this about your mom?"

"My mother never got a chance to *live*." She wanted to take back the words as soon as she uttered them. But it was too late.

Hank leaned against the headboard, his posture open, his eyes clear and sweet and strong. What would it feel like to crawl back into bed? To lean on him?

"And..." he prompted.

She found her underwear next to the bedside table and pulled them on. "She died of cancer so young—she'd never done anything but get married and have us. Not one other thing."

"So you think you have to live for her. I can see that. But is it fair? Is that what she would want?"

"Of course she would. She regretted everything she'd never done. Her last words..." *See it all. Do it all.* Samantha had tried to follow her mother's directive. It was even why she'd initially learned how to fight. Her mother had always wanted to do judo or taekwondo, but her body had never been strong enough. Samantha had studied the moves— even when she wasn't doing well in her own life, even when she was training through a vodka haze—so she could make her dead mother proud.

"Would she want you to take a chance on love?"

If Samantha loved, if she stayed in place, her roots would grow, and maybe she wouldn't do all the things she needed to do for her mother. Her head felt fuzzy. That was true, right? That's what she'd believed for so long...

Hank stayed still as he said, "I'm taking a chance here. With you. I think we could do this, Samantha. I really do."

"But you can't take a chance on anything else."

"I don't need to."

"No one *lives* if they don't risk."

"Samantha." Hank's voice was scratchy and low. "There's this quote that says you should jump of the cliff and build your wings on the way down. I'm risking everything. Right now. Can't you see that? You've changed me. I'm jumping off the cliff. Hoping I have wings."

Samantha pulled on the jeans she'd finally dragged out from under the bed and dug an elastic out of the pocket. She pulled back her hair viciously and twisted it into a ponytail. "Prove it."

"What?"

"Do something dangerous."

He frowned, and crossed his arms. "I don't get it."

"Show me you've changed. That you can live on the edge." *That you can fly with those wings.*

"Telling you I love you isn't enough?"

She wanted it to be. "They're just words. Do something scary and risky."

"You understand that my job, my whole way of life, is about mitigating danger."

That was what she was worried about. Samantha tossed her ponytail over her shoulder and raised her chin, wishing for her glasses to hide behind. "*I'm* danger. How would you mitigate me?"

"I won't. I promise."

"You'll try to. They all do." She pulled on her jacket and picked up her bag from where she'd flung it in the corner. "*Damn*, I want a drink."

Hank's eyes went wide. "You don't."

She gave him one final look, aching with how she would miss what this could have been. What it should have been. "I always do. That's the thing. But not having a drink is something I have to accomplish myself. Alone. You can't help. I wish you could. You can't save me, Hank, and you can't make me safe." *I love you anyway.*

She couldn't say the words.

It wouldn't be fair to him. And in her leaving, she needed to be fair. If she could, she would choose him. If she could have what she wanted, she would curl up in his arms and let him take care of her, let him make her safe.

But that didn't work. She'd seen firsthand what it looked like when a woman loved a man so much she was willing to give everything else in the world up. Samantha's mother had given her whole life to their father, and then, when she'd gotten sick, she had nothing to draw from. No memories of dancing on beaches, no recollections of long Sunday mornings in bed with various lovers. Her mother didn't know what language they spoke in Brazil, or what coffee tasted like in Italy. Of course, her mother also hadn't had any idea what it was like to be detoxing in a tiny motel just outside Phoenix with five dollars in nickels stashed an old Altoids tin, with no cell phone, no one within a thousand miles that knew her middle name.

Hank's dark, bruised-looking eyes made her want to cry. "Don't go," he said one last time. "Stay with me."

So he could put her in box and keep her safe. Keep her from *burning*, from living her life with fire and flame and verve and lust and excitement. No, she was too much her mother's daughter to let that ever happen. She would never be her mother, coddled and protected by a man who, in the end, could save her from nothing.

And more than that, she was enough her mother's daughter to not allow herself to hurt this man again. She'd done it once to him. Once was enough, and if she stayed a little longer, she'd hurt him deeper by not staying, by not choosing the safe road. For the first time, she realized that if she'd stepped off the back of that motorcycle years ago, choosing Hank back then, she wouldn't be the person she was today.

And he wouldn't be the Hank she loved.

Samantha could only think of one thing to say that would make it better, and they were the words she couldn't give him. So she dropped her gaze to the floor and left, closing the door softly behind her as she went.

CHAPTER 20

HANK TOOK ANOTHER body-blow. The women were getting better with throwing punches, and they were all excited to get their turn on him instead of the bag Samantha had hung from a rafter. Kelly, especially, was really getting into it. He was sorry Wally wasn't here today to take some of the jabs for him, but he'd had something to do with his daughter.

"That's it, Kelly! Harder! Don't let him push you like that by the shoulders! Remember what we worked on with the twist and elbow." Samantha's voice was professional and just the right tone and pitch. Just as it had been for the last two weeks.

Two weeks of this awful, broken silence. Samantha was cordial when they worked with the class together. Afterward, she always ushered him to the community center door along with the last couple of students, thanking him kindly for coming, for doing such a great job.

He was nothing to her, that was what her carefully upright body telegraphed. Her voice told him that he was a valued part of her teaching sessions, nothing more.

But her eyes said something different to him, and at least twice a class, Hank was tempted to hurl himself at her in his padded suit and let her whale on him until that bleak, haunted look in the back of that green gaze abated.

He didn't do it, though. He just did his job in the class. He was the attacker. The women, his victims, were becoming friends while his helmet was off.

Samantha, though, smiled at him like they were only slightly acquainted. Hank had kissed her, loved her with his fingers and mouth and body and mind until she'd wept in his arms with release, and just this afternoon, when she'd held the community center's door open for him, she'd looked as if she was considering whether or not to put him on her Christmas card list.

"Harder!" yelled Samantha. "Come on, Kelly, you can hit him harder than that."

"*Oof.*" Yeah, he was definitely off her list. He held his arms up, his signal for defeat. He'd pushed Kelly into a corner and pinned her down, using everything Samantha had taught him, and she'd gotten away from him and then kicked his butt. There were still two classes to go in this course, and Kelly was going to be the star pupil, he could tell. She loved fighting and winning. And her sisters, while doing well themselves, *loved* watching her, cheering her loudly.

It would have been uplifting if he hadn't been getting so pummeled by fists and shoulders and knees and feet. The suit was good, and he'd learned a little bit about how to block, but he'd be bruised tomorrow. The pain almost felt like some kind of relief.

He'd blown it.

Hank had lost her.

As Linda got into place on the mat, he looked through

the mesh of the helmet at Samantha. She stood tall at the edge of the fighting area, her shoulders drawn back. Her cheeks were pale, and for a second, he saw something in her face waver. Then she bit her lip quickly and the look was gone. She was all business again.

"Linda, you have this."

Linda did *not* have this. Hank could tell she was on the verge of tears. He made a time-out sign with his hands and lifted off his helmet, tucking it under his arm. "Hey," he said, stepping toward her. "You want to take a minute?"

"No," she muttered, looking at the plastic blue mat beneath her bare feet.

"It's me," he said. "It's Hank."

"No," she said again in a low voice. "You're the bad guy." She looked up into Hank's face and instantly burst into tears, running off toward the bathroom.

He turned to face Samantha. "Crap," he said. "Sorry."

Samantha frowned.

And then a blast rocked the room.

CHAPTER 21

GLASS FLEW FROM the window behind Samantha as she fell to her knees. She heard Gina scream, and then heard thumps as things fell from the shelves in the storage room.

Earthquake? No, an earthquake jolted and rolled—it wasn't a blast like that had been.

From outside the now smashed window, she heard a hissing noise, and then a series of pops, similar to but louder than her stove made when it didn't want to light. She saw a jet of flame from the sidewalk and then another one join it in the middle of the street. She bit back her own cry. There wasn't time to freak out. She had to get her students to safety.

"Back door," she yelled.

Hank had already ripped off his padded suit, and had the back door propped open in seconds.

"I'm getting Linda," he said to her. "Keep everyone behind the building. Go toward whatever's not smoking. I'm right behind you."

"What do you—"

"Gas line rupture. Has to be."

Now she could smell it, the sulfuric odor of natural gas.

And if she could smell it, that meant it was in the air. If it was in the air, it could blow...

"Go!" she urged Dot and Kayla. "Move your feet. Everyone *out*. Hank's getting Linda."

She herded the seven women outside, looking over her shoulder as she went through the door. The front windows were gone, and on the other side of them, where they could usually see cars and parking meters, she could see sheets of flame that leapt and receded. "Hank!"

"I'm coming," he called. He came through the side door from the bathroom, his arm around Linda's waist. She was bleeding from the forehead.

"What happened?"

Linda touched her face with her fingertips as Hank led her out the back door. "I fell. What's burning? What's on fire?"

Hank looked over his shoulder. "The whole damn world, I think."

THE BACK SIDE of the building opened into a parking lot, and Hank was in no way sure that they were far enough away from the gas line rupture. The whole block could go at any minute, if it was a transmission line failure. He racked his brain to remember the PSI of the line that ran under First Street. A trans line ran through town, the kind of line that blew up to 900 PSI, the same as the line that had blown under San Bruno a few years before. That blast had taken out thirty-five houses and killed eight people. Other lower PSI distribution lines ran through Darling Bay, but try as he could, Hank couldn't bring the map into his mind. He needed to be in the back of the rig, where he kept his own set of pre-plans in a plastic box he loaded into the engine at the beginning and end of each shift. Other guys laughed at him—there were generic pre-plans in each engine—but Hank worried about the one day they were going somewhere and they weren't there, removed by admin for an update or a careless firefighter who didn't remember to put them back. So he carried his own.

Fat lot of good that would do him now.

One thing he hoped he remembered correctly—that the lines near the water were the low-pressure ones. "Keep going," he yelled. "Toward the marina. Go, go!" With one hand he fumbled with his cell phone, keeping his other arm around Linda who felt so limp he was worried she was going to pass out. He called dispatch, the inside line. "Lexie. What is it?"

"I don't have time, Hank," the dispatcher blurted. He could hear every 911 line ringing in the background.

"I'm on First near Lincoln."

"Get *out*," she said. "Can you?"

"Not the way we came. We're headed to the water."

He heard the clicking of her keyboard. "How many?"

"Nine of us."

"I've got three engines and two trucks on the way—get to the second pier on the curve. Barger's setting up IC. He just got on scene."

"Gas breach?"

"We think so. Be safe." She hung up without saying goodbye.

Hank led the way down First to the pier, herding the women as best be could. He couldn't be both in front of and in back of them—he couldn't protect them on all sides. He needed there to be five of him, but instead, there was only one.

There was a thump to the southeast as something—probably a car or a personal propane tank—blew, and Linda screamed. Samantha let go of Kelly and came to take Linda's other hand.

Samantha's voice was perfect. "You can do this," she said. "We have you. Hank and I are going to keep you safe, okay?"

Tears coursed down Linda's face, but she nodded. They were almost to the dock where Chief Barger was setting up incident command.

"Get behind the engine, on the other side. As far away from the—" Hank broke off as they all saw what was happening together.

Flames. Rising from each crack in the pavement, from every manhole in the street. Not big flames, just small licking red ones. Tentative ones.

Holy crap. The street itself was *on fire*.

The best place would be on the pier itself. "On the dock itself, on the wood, get off the pavement," he said.

"What if the dock burns?" Gina's voice shook.

"It won't." Hank had no idea if it would or not. "But if it does, swim."

Samantha met his eyes for a heartbeat, and Hank tried to say with his gaze what he was feeling—that he wanted to take her—just her—and wrap her up, lead her to where she'd be safe, and then...

Then she broke the gaze and threw herself into herding the group to the dock. "Come on, let's go, let's go. Those fast feet you had on the mat? Move 'em now. Let me see you run."

She was taking care of herself and those around her. Of course.

Barger was already in the middle of doing sixteen things when Hank ran up to him. He was yelling into the radio clipped to his shoulder, and the other radio was held to his ear. He'd already unrolled the PG&E map and was staring at the lines on the grid while he marked notes on the whiteboard on the open door of his SUV.

"Where do you want me, boss?"

Barger barely glanced at him. "No PPEs? Just stay out of the way."

He didn't have his personal protective equipment because he wasn't on duty. His civvies wouldn't protect him from fire, but he could still be of use. "You evacuating? I can help the cops with the knock and talk." He was fast and because he wasn't loaded down with gear, he could move more quickly than the cops or the other firefighters could. "Which blocks?"

"Out. And don't move a muscle in the direction of the fire."

The flames were still licking up from the street. None of the buildings on First Street had caught yet, but if the gas wasn't capped soon, they all would, and Hank knew there was no way their small department could prevent major loss. It would take half an hour for mutual aid to roll into town, and by then, half of downtown Darling Bay could be lost.

Maureen. But no, his grandmother would be safe if she was at home—that was almost a mile away, and she was always home this time of day, just before dinner.

More and more sirens filled the air—engines, ambulances and trucks headed their way, and over the top of the noise whined the volunteer siren. Lexie and whoever was with her in dispatch would have started the entire department this way, along with the fifty or so volunteers that would come running when they heard the recall. Of course, *they* would have their PPEs cleverly stowed in their cars. The nearest station where he might find some was six blocks away, and he wasn't leaving Samantha alone for long enough to run and grab them.

Samantha. She wasn't on the dock with the students anymore. His head swiveled as he tried to catch sight of her ponytail bobbing somewhere in the crowd of people who were lining themselves up on the safe side of the street, the one bounded by water. Skip Lemon raced out of his ice cream shop and leaped a low line of flame, raising gasps from the onlookers. Barger yelled, "Anyone else in there?"

"Hardware store and the pizzeria are all clear. Monty's checking the library, and the bar was closed, we think."

Samantha. Where the *hell* was Samantha?

Tox, also off duty, but damn his eyes, dressed in his PPEs, race-walked Grace Rowe to the same pier where Samantha's class waited.

Hank grabbed Grace's elbow. "Have you seen your sister?"

Grace's eyes widened in horror. "No. She had her class —I thought she'd be here." She looked down the block, to where the road curved. They could just see the bagel shop.

"Would she—" It was a dumb question. Hank didn't even have to finishing asking it. Of course she would.

Hank took off at a run.

CHAPTER 22

I T WAS STUPID, she knew that. She was going to catch hell from Hank later.

But Gus was on the sidewalk—Gus who had come back from his Costa Rica trip only because he loved his cat so much. He was wringing his hands, looking across the low, flickering flames toward the bagel store, and above it, his apartment. On his balcony next to her own, she could just make out the large orange shape of Anchor.

It was taking both Johannes and Pastor Jacobs to hold him back and keep him from running across the street.

But Gus wouldn't make it if Anchor didn't. That cat was all Gus had left in the world.

And no one was holding Samantha back.

All of First Street was on fire. Not the buildings, not yet, but Samantha assumed that it wasn't long until they caught. Now it was just ripples of flame shooting up from cracks in the sidewalk and from the grates at the edge of street. And there were gaps in the flame.

She was fast. Samantha had always been fast.

A good block before her apartment, a block before

anyone with Gus caught sight of her, Samantha raced between two jets of fire. *Move, keep moving, don't slip, don't fall, don't stand still.*

It was hotter than she could have imagined. She picked a good gap to run through, at least ten feet from the nearest burst of flame, but even then, the heat was intense. Her cheeks and the exposed skin on her arms hurt. The air was full of dark black smoke and smelled of chemicals and something blacker, tar or creosote. Behind her, safe in their berths, the boats' masts clanked as if nothing was wrong. The sun was setting, an orange dusk lowering, just like any other day in Darling Bay. The birds were gone, though. No seagulls floated above—there were no scattered cries.

Samantha heard shouting, and ran harder. Almost there, almost there...

The photo album. The one with the pictures of her and Grace as children in the Valley, their parents still smiling, her mother not yet in pain. She could get it, once she got to the building.

But she didn't think she could carry both an enormous squirming cat and the heavy photo album—not both and still get back through the flames safely. Almost as quickly as she'd thought of it, she gave up the hope of saving the album.

Really, it wasn't important.

When she got to the building, Anchor wasn't on the balcony any more. He must have gone inside. Samantha barreled around the building to the back staircase. She had Gus's key on her ring, and she raced up the back steps so fast she stumbled on the top one.

Gus's lock stuck as it always did. *Not now, please.* She hit the door with her shoulder and the lock finally twisted. Inside, though, the orange beast was visible nowhere.

"Anchor? Here, kitty-kitty." As if that cat had ever done a single thing anyone had ever wanted him to.

Maybe he'd gone from Gus's balcony to hers? She often left her French doors open, and more than once, she'd found Anchor sleeping smack-dab in the middle of her favorite pillow.

She tore out of Gus's apartment and into her own.

She'd just shut the door behind her when the explosion happened.

THE HEAT WAS A ROAR. An inferno.

And it was coming from behind the bagel store. From near the staircase Samantha must have just gone up.

Hank had no fear, no nervousness—he felt nothing other than a complete, total urgency to get there, get to her, get there *now*. Something was preventing him, though. He yanked his arm as hard as he could, trying to get free.

"No," roared Barger in his ear. "You're not going anywhere near that building. It's gonna light up in about a second."

"That's why I'm going," Hank said calmly to his boss. "Samantha's there."

"I don't care if my mama's in there, you're not going." Barger increased the pressure on Hank's arm. "Tox! Get over here! Hold this guy!"

Oh, no. Tox was a beast. He was huge. If Tox got hold of him, Hank wouldn't have a chance.

He straightened and put on as calm a face as he could. "Understood, sir. Where can you best use me, given that I don't have my PPEs?"

"Good man," said Barger, releasing him. "I need a pair of eyes for safety on the corner of Lowry and First…"

But Hank was gone. Whatever secondary fuel supply had just blown behind the bagel shop wouldn't give Samantha much time to get out. And in the whole town, in the whole world, there was only one person he needed to save.

Samantha.

He broke through the fire at Taylor where two fountains of flame sputtered. Maybe whatever underground tank had caught was running out of gas? If it were storage, that would make sense, but not if it was an incoming distribution line. If was incoming, it could get even worse, and fast. He darted toward the back of the bagel shop, but the heat was too intense. If he went to her staircase was, the super-heated gas would rip into his lungs.

He had to get her *out* of here.

The front of the building was the only way to go. When the kid had fallen off the rock, Hank had gone down by climbing the drain pipe—he could go up it now.

Hand over hand, carefully placing his feet square on the wall so they didn't slip, Hank pulled himself up. One long reach and he pulled himself over the balcony's rail. From inside her apartment, and from the one next door, curled wisps of black smoke. The roof, then, had caught. In a minute, maybe less, the entire building would be burning.

Inside, he found her down on the kitchen floor. The smoke had taken her out. Not dead. *Not dead.* She couldn't be dead. Frantically, he pushed his fingers against her throat. He found her pulse, still strong. Relief tasted like sugar in his soot-filled mouth.

Hank grabbed the nearest two pillowcases and shook them free of their pillows. He wrapped one around her face and then one around his. It wouldn't do much to prevent the gas inhalation, but it would help with the heat, at least. Scanning the apartment, he caught sight of the blankets on the back of the couch. Perfect. Wool. Wool was naturally fire retardant.

He wrapped one afghan around his body as best he could, then he pulled the other one around her prone body. She held something soft and heavy in her hands—the cat. She'd come back for her neighbor's *cat*. Well, at least it was unconscious, too, and wouldn't present much of a problem to carry out, if he bundled it inside his blanket. Hank's hands fumbled as he attempted to tighten the blanket around Samantha's arms, her hair. If he didn't hurry, he too would be unconscious in about thirty seconds, if he didn't get them all out of here right *now*. Unceremoniously, he shoved the cat into his blanket, using it like a Snugli, the way women at Mabel's Cafe did in the mornings.

Then he slung Samantha over his shoulder in a fireman's carry.

He put his hand on her door. Too hot.

It was way too hot.

He'd be lucky if the stairs were even still there. If they weren't there, then he and Samantha weren't getting out of this place alive, not with active fire surrounding the block it sat on.

It was against every protocol in the book to open the door to her stairs. It would have been better for him to go out the French doors and drop her off the balcony, following her over. But he couldn't protect her that way, couldn't guarantee that she'd fall the right way, that she wouldn't land on her head and die instantly—or worse, die later, slowly, after a painful injury.

Damn it all. The whole block could ignite any second.

It could go up like San Bruno had. There was no time to waste, *none*.

Hank tore open the door, ignoring the initial blast of heat he felt against his face. The entire parking lot behind the building was on fire—even the pavement was burning. Four or five cars were fully involved, but miraculously, the stairs were just starting to singe from the heat and weren't actively on fire yet.

He ran toward the water with her. He ran toward dusk's sunset faster than he'd ever run on any fire department test, faster than when he'd been sprinting 5ks every weekend. He ran faster through the heat than he'd ever run with the work dummy over his shoulder. He raced so fast over a plume of flame that shot out of the pavement that the wool they were wrapped in didn't even scorch.

But Hank wasn't running as if his life depended on it, even though it did.

He was running as if hers did, and that was the source of his speed.

CHAPTER 23

A N OLD MAN Hank didn't know was at his elbow, tugging.

"You saved his life. You saved his life."

Hank looked down at the grass where Samantha lay. Smoke from the smoldering asphalt blew across them. PG&E had capped the gas line, and there was no more active fuel for the fire, but the fire department was just now attempting to fight the two active blazes—the bagel shop and Skip's Ice Cream. Usually, Hank would do anything to fight any one of those fires. On a normal day, there would be *nothing* that would keep him away from helping his department and his community.

Today? With her lying in front of him, that mane of hair tangled and dark with soot, Barger could have offered him a million dollars and a promotion to deputy chief and he would have quit before leaving her side.

Not that Barger would have. Mutual aid engines and trucks from Eureka had arrived, along with a fleet of ambulances to treat the injured. Darling Bay would lose the two buildings, but it had lost buildings to fire before. Hank hated that Samantha would wake to find her home—and her second job—gone, but at least she was here. With him.

"*Her* life," he corrected the old man. "Yeah, she'll be okay."

Chaos swirled around them—parents rushing to find their kids who'd been hanging out after school at the marina, news vans who'd crawled out of the woodwork the moment "gas fire" had been said on the radio. People were yelling, crying.

None of it mattered.

Samantha would be okay—just fine to live her life, to leave and start new elsewhere, because when did someone like Samantha settle down, really? He was just lucky she'd stayed as long as she had.

"No, *his* life," insisted the man. He gestured at the orange blanket under his arm. Only it wasn't a blanket.

"Anchor. That's *your* cat."

"I'm Gus. The girl has told me plenty about you."

"She has?"

"Yup. You're all she talks about."

"Anything I want to know?" Probably not. Most likely, what Samantha told her neighbor was about what a close call she'd had. Maybe she'd even confessed that she'd made a man fall in love with her twice, the second time about a billion times worse than the first.

Gus shrugged. "It's hard when you're in love with someone."

"Thanks, man, but you can keep your pity."

Gus looked startled, but only said, "Are you the one who brought my cat back to life?"

He was, actually. Bonnie Maddern, one of their medics, hadn't let him touch Samantha when he got her out of fire danger. *You can't. You're too close to her. Get out of my way. I mean it, Coffee. You're on thin enough ice with Barger as it is. He said he'll have your badge by the end of the day. Go fix that cat you dragged out.*

Fine, Hank had thought while giving the cat oxygen and massaging its chest. Barger could take his badge, but Hank would know for the rest of his life that Samantha had lived because of him. She would be dead right now—Hank had given a choked cry as the cat stretched and yawned under his hands. She wasn't dead. The cat, too, was alive. "Anchor," he'd said. "Anchor. You're back. You son of a bitch."

"Yeah," Hank said now to Gus. "I did bring him back to life."

"Samantha said you didn't take no risks."

"Normally I don't." He stood taller to look over the short man's shoulder. On the lawn, Bonnie was still attending to Samantha. She was talking now. Awake. He saw her sit up halfway and then be encouraged by Bonnie to lie down flat again. How were her lungs? What was her O2 sat now? What if Bonnie didn't keep a close enough eye on it?

"Anchor and I thank you."

"Why do you call him Anchor?" Anything to take his mind off Samantha and his need to rush to her side.

"I was a sailor, see." Gus grinned. "That's funny. See, sea, get it?"

"I get it," said Hank shortly.

"I met this girl when I put in to Darling Bay in my boat. Well, you know, I fell in love. I was young. Okay, younger than I am now. I was sixty-eight when Sheila and I met. She was younger, only sixty. A looker, too. Did you know her? Sheila Westin, from just north of the harbor?"

Hank shook his head, barely able to focus on the man's words. Samantha was sitting up all the way now, moving her hands as if she was arguing with Bonnie about getting up. Uh-uh. Bonnie better *not* let her up. He put one hand on Gus's shoulder. "I don't think I knew her. I should get over there—"

"You listen to me just one goldarntootin' minute, you hear me?" Under Gus's arm, Anchor hissed as if on cue. "I got something to say to you."

"Okay?"

"She's in love with you, and she's terrified that she's not good enough for you."

The middle of Hank's stomach lurched. "For *me*? I'm not good enough for *her*."

"Yeah," said Gus, nodding. "She's worried about that, too. That's what I'm trying to say. I didn't think I could take care of Sheila on my pension, what with how much money I blew on my boat every year. She didn't want to be with a sailor—she hated water. And the fact that I was allergic to cats was the capper. I left. Sailed away.

"By the time I turned around at the Farrallons and sailed back, she was gone. She went into the hospital with a stomachache and left dead of a cancer she didn't know about till the end. She had time to write a will on the back of a hospital tissue box, and she left me this damn cat right here. Anchor, she told me to call him. Because this cat was my anchor to this place, to her memory." Gus swabbed his lower lip with a purple-checked handkerchief. "What she didn't know was that I was already on my way back to her side. I was never gonna leave her again. And I guess, in my way, I haven't." He hoisted the cat rear-end first, waving his luxurious tail in Hank's direction. "I'm saying go to her, you fool boy. What if you can change her mind? You have that chance. Take it. I never had mine."

Hank stared at the old man for a second. Then he turned and ran toward Samantha.

From behind him floated Gus's quavery voice. "Just kiss her, boy! Don't be an idiot!"

CHAPTER 24

S AMANTHA CLOSED HER eyes and concentrating on stilling her breathing. Her lungs hurt, but not too badly. It felt as if she'd never get the smell of smoke out of her nose, and she knew it would stay in her hair for weeks. She was freezing, too. Dusk had almost fully dropped, and the already cold day was turning to ice as the cold ocean air pushed its way inland. It was clear tonight, no fog, making it even colder. Samantha saw one star struggle to draw breath as the sunset reddened the sky.

Bonnie Maddern was nice enough. She'd started to tell Samantha how she'd gotten out of her apartment, but then she'd been called away by a man in uniform with a huge mustache and a booming voice.

Oh, her poor beloved apartment. The one that Hank had thought she would burn down with her crappy extension cords. If she looked over her right shoulder, she could see it, a blackened hull, the fire now out, having left little behind. Her heart ached for Johannes—the bagel shop was all he had. She hoped his insurance would let him rebuild.

Her photo album. The only remaining pictures of their

parents, gone. She'd only been borrowing them from Grace —they'd talked about making copies at some point, or digitizing them, and they hadn't gotten around to it yet. Now they never would. Her mother. She'd never see her mother again.

It hurt too much to cry.

The man with the loud voice stood next to her. She shaded her eyes against the low sun behind him.

"You okay, ma'am?"

"I think so," said Samantha. "For having just lost my home."

From behind her came Hank's voice. "You can stay with me."

Samantha swiveled her head, her heart lifting ridiculously high—sleeping in his bed, touching him, being with him—before it dropped again. "No, thanks."

"We can talk about it," said Hank. "After you get a good night's rest. At my place."

She shut her eyes, opening them again only reluctantly. "You're too bossy."

"He is," growled the tall man who was obviously both the boss and in a terrible mood. Samantha supposed if she'd just had to fight an entire block's worth of fire, she'd be grumpy too.

"You're fired, Coffee," said the man. "You are so damn fired. Sorry, ma'am."

"Oh, don't be," said Samantha, waving a hand. "I fire him all the time, too."

"You can't fire me, Chief," said Hank cheerfully. "I just saved her life." He pointed at Samantha.

Ah. So that's how she'd gotten out. She should have known. "Anchor! Did he get out? Where's Gus's cat?"

The chief paid her no attention. "You broke every rule

in the book, Coffee, and considering that you've personally worked on rewriting most of the policies in that book, that's pretty shocking. We'll take this up in the after-action report but you blatantly disregarded the safety of our department, our citizens, and yourself."

Samantha's jaw dropped. "You broke a rule?"

Hank nodded. "Yep. A bunch of 'em."

"All of them. In order to get you to safety, ma'am."

Samantha could see the chief almost biting his lip not to insult a member of the community. It was okay, though, she could take the criticism. "It was my fault, sir. I ran across the street to try to save my neighbor's cat." She pressed her fingers to her lips. "Oh, *Anchor*. He was Gus's girlfriend's cat. I wish..."

"I saved him, too," said Hank, looking even brighter.

"You *did?*"

The chief said in a low voice, "You saved a *cat?*"

"Yep. You think the media has that yet?"

Groaning, the chief said, "A *cat*. I'll never be able to fire you. Ever. Damn you to hell, Coffee." He stalked away, his gait stiff.

Hank dropped into a cross-legged position next to her on the grass. "Well, I guess we handled *that*."

Samantha tried to speak, but ended up coughing instead.

Hank's lightness disappeared. "We need Bonnie back here. Why didn't she transport you to the hospital already?"

"I told her I'm not going. Tell me about the rules you broke."

A smile played across his lips, and that muscle jumped in his jaw. Samantha's fingers ached to reach out and touch it—but she couldn't. How could she trust herself to touch him and then let him go again?

"What *didn't* I do wrong? I disobeyed my chief to stay out of the way. I went through a fire line without protective equipment. I scaled a building up a drain pipe because the stairs were too dangerous, and then, when I couldn't get you down that way, I took you out the dangerous way, wrapped in blankets. When we got back through the flames again, your blanket was on fire, and I beat it out with my hands."

"You did?" She noticed for the first time that both his hands were bandaged. "*Hank.*"

He held them out as if surprised by them. "They're fine. You know what? I prayed. The whole way down your steps, I prayed, and Samantha, I'm not a religious man. I haven't prayed since my grandmother got sick a few years ago and we thought we were going to lose her. What I did could have killed you." His voice wobbled, and his eyes squinted, as if the sun had gotten suddenly brighter. "I could have killed you instead of saving you. I can't believe I did that."

"I guess this means your prayers work."

"They don't."

Samantha stayed quiet. It was his moment to speak. She'd had her moment, when she'd closed his bedroom door. She'd said all she needed to say by not looking at him every time they worked with her students, when she was the only one in class who didn't touch him. She couldn't. She'd been using Wally to demonstrate the moves, and if he wasn't there, she'd been describing them verbally, praying her students didn't notice the way her knees shook when Hank got too close to her.

Hank continued, "If my prayers worked, you never would have gotten on the back of Vicente's motorcycle that night. If my prayers were any good, I would have figured out the words to make you stay with me, where you belonged."

Where she belonged... How could the words feel so right? And yet...

"If my prayers worked," he said, "you would have been in my bed every night all these years. You wouldn't have hurt yourself with the things you did, and I wouldn't have wasted so much time looking for a woman who was anything like you. Trouble, there's no one like you anywhere in the whole world. I could hire a flock of monks or a battalion of priests to pray around the clock, and I'd never run across someone I loved the way I love you."

"Oh." The word was a breath.

"You can't be with me because you don't want to give up your dreams. If you give up your dreams, you let down your mother, do I have that right?"

It sounded small, almost silly, when he put it so simply. But it wasn't small or simple at all. It was who she was. She had to *do* more than just exist.

He dug in the back pocket of his jeans and pulled out an envelope. "Water bill," he said. "It'll do. Hey, Bonnie! You got a pen?"

The medic looked up from where she was bandaging a little girl's arm. She gave a long-arm toss and threw Hank the pen that was in her shirt front pocket.

"Here," he said, thrusting the pen and paper at her. "Write them down."

"What?"

"Your dreams. All of them. Write 'em down for me."

"Hank..." But something started to grow inside her, a green tendril of hope uncurling, slowly.

"Write."

She made a list. She handed the folded envelope to him.

He read it, tiny wrinkles creasing at the corners of his

eyes. "Okay. Uh-huh. Yeah, okay. Yes." He nodded with each word.

"What? You think all of that's possible?"

Looking at the paper, Hank said, "Climbing the side of a volcano? Bungee-jumping in New Zealand? Riding the Trans-Siberian railway? You think we *can't* do all this? Have I mentioned that not only do I get four days off a week, but I have two months of vacation a year and I can get trades for up to four more months? And they pay me well for this gig, not sure if you knew that. I'll order my passport online as soon as I get home and pull these bandages off."

"What about the other things?" Samantha's heart beat so hard she was sure he would hear it, even over the chaos around them.

She saw his Adam's apple bob as he swallowed. "*Have a baby.* That one I can't quite manage on my own." He looked directly into her eyes, and the warm coffee of them melted her heart. "Maybe you'd be able to help me with that someday."

"Someday, maybe," she said, breathless. "That's a someday-maybe list."

He nodded, looking back down at the envelope. "I like the getting married one, too. Again, I'd need help with that."

"I'm actually kind of good with helping people," Samantha said. "Not as good as you are, but..."

"I need to know this, though."

Samantha nodded, the green tendril of hope inside her quaking.

"Are you brave enough to choose someone safe?"

That was the question. That was what she'd been trying to answer, and she hadn't even known how to put it into words.

Safety.

It was the most dangerous thing of all. To risk her heart on someone who was steady. In place. Someone who wasn't going anywhere, or at least, not going anywhere without her.

Samantha had never been so terrified in all her life.

But she knew the answer.

"Yes. I think I'm exactly that brave."

The paper fluttered out of his hands, and he was kissing her then, his mouth firm and hot on hers, and Samantha was kissing him back. She tasted salt and ash, and she didn't know whose tears were in her mouth—it just mattered that his arms were around her, and she could finally, *finally* come home. And stay there.

CHAPTER 25

THE ATTACKER BARRELED out of a side door, his prey the small, bird-like woman who perched nervously in the folding chair. She screamed when he knocked her to the ground, and the group watching the attack gasped collectively.

Samantha, watching closely, couldn't help noticing that the people in the audience who were having the hardest time weren't the family members of the women who were graduating, but the ten firefighters who'd come to watch Hank demonstrate what he did on his days off. Each one of them was wound so tight that Samantha wouldn't risk touching any of them—they might explode like that gas line had last month. When Wally had tested Kelly, they'd started the fight with her pinned against the wall in exactly the position she'd been pinned when she was raped in the bathroom of her bar. Pre-scripted, he said the same ugly words to her that the man had said then. Standing in the audience, Kelly's sisters bounced on the balls of their toes as if they wanted to elbow their way in and fight for her. But they understood that Kelly had to fight her own way out.

The firefighters might have understood that mentally, but physically, at a base level, it was obvious they hated this. To a man, they were twitching. One had let out an outraged bellow when the first student had been knocked over by her attacker. Tox had his hands balled at his sides, and Coin kept moving toward the mat, only drawing back when his girlfriend Lexie took his hand. These were men who ran toward the problem. They were men who, when something blew up, turned around and hurled their bodies at the fire to put it out instead of running away like average people. When someone was threatened, they moved to help without even thinking, and watching women have to fight their way out of an attack, alone, was almost killing them. Samantha had already seen a couple brush away angry, emotional tears.

Tears were normal during a graduation. Emotions were high, for everyone involved.

Especially for Linda McCracken, who hadn't managed yet to win a fight. In all cases, Hank or Wally had to stop because she gave up, curling into a ball on the floor, refusing to fight back. Samantha was going to let her graduate with the rest of the class tonight because she deserved it, but she'd keep working with her after this until Linda had successfully used the power of her body to stop a full-strength attack.

Hank didn't hold back, even though just that morning, he'd confessed to Samantha that he could barely bear to fight her anymore. "It's like beating up a child. I'm not sure I can be that guy anymore. Even though she's paying you, and you're paying me."

"Maybe if you would cash a single check I've made out to you, you could make that complaint. But until you do..."

He'd smiled but persisted. "Tonight will be the last time

I fight her. If she doesn't win, then she'll have to train with Wally. I can't take it anymore."

"You're helping her," reminded Samantha.

He'd shaken his head. "I know that, mentally. But physically, I can't do it to her anymore. Tonight's the last time."

Now, Samantha could tell that Hank wasn't holding back on the mat. He had Linda pinned to the ground, and she was stuck. She was thrashing too much—how many times had Samantha gone over that with her? Linda was wasting her precious physical and mental energy fighting that way and she was getting nowhere.

Fight smart, not hard. Samantha willed Linda to remember. *Smart, not hard.*

Then Linda stilled, gathering herself. A head butt—a hard one, followed by an elbow jab, thrown from the ground. Then Linda burst into a flurry of short, very sharp kicks, kicks that would have broken Hank's leg if he weren't wearing the suit. Hank must have known it too, because he slowed.

Her teeth bared, Linda screamed the most important two words Samantha taught: "*Stop. No!*" Linda scrambled to her feet, but so did Hank. He caught her arm roughly, yanking her to him, but Linda—without seeming to think—drew her knee up, hitting him in the groin. With a groan that was probably pretty real, Hank dropped. Linda raced to stand at his head, something she'd never been able to do before.

"No means *no!*" she yelled.

All around her, the audience roared, "Down and *out!*"

Hank was down, Linda was out, running off the mat, toward Samantha.

Samantha wrapped her arms around the small, shaking woman. "You did it. You really *did* it."

Linda hiccupped a sob and nodded. "I did. I *did*."

Hank took off his helmet and came toward them. Linda launched herself at him, but this time in a hug. "Thank you. Thank you," she said.

Samantha heard more sniffling from the crowd and knew hers weren't the only tears flowing.

From next to her, a woman said, "Yeah, well, he did pretty good, too."

Maureen, Hank's grandmother, had sidled up next to Samantha. She stood knitting in place, a striped green sock dangling from two circular needles.

"He did," agreed Samantha.

"I never taught him to attack women."

"I think you taught him the opposite."

"So this—" Maureen flapped the sock at the crowd. "This is what you do now? Instead of drinking?"

"This is my addiction." *This and Hank.*

"Huh. I used to smoke before I took up knitting. Maybe sometimes we just have to switch a bad one for a good one. My first husband was no good so I got a better one, just for one example."

"I like your style."

Hank came up behind them. Maureen threw a fake jab with her elbow backward. "I can take you, young man."

"You know I can teach you, too, if you want to learn," said Samantha.

"I'd be scared of that. Gramma doesn't need help in beating anyone up. She never has." Hank caught Maureen's elbow lightly and then slipped an arm around them both. "How are my two favorite women?"

Maureen peeked her head around Hank's chest at Samantha. "I'd say we're tolerable."

"Yeah," said Samantha, feeling that by-now familiar

kick of joy in her chest. "Tolerable's just about right." She looked around the room—her sister Grace was laughing with Tox at the doorway. Earlier, during Gina's fight, Grace had grabbed Samantha's hand and whispered in her ear, "Mom would be as proud of you as I am."

If she hadn't been so focused on Gina, Samantha would have wept.

Now Linda was talking earnestly with Gus near the water dispenser, and a cluster of firefighters were reading Samantha's brochure, talking about which of their wives should take the class first.

Samantha had built this. In one place, with her two hands and the scrap of an idea, Samantha had built this for herself.

And when it came to love? Samantha had leaped off the cliff, unfurling the wings she hadn't known she had.

So yeah, things were tolerable if that meant being in love with the sexiest, sweetest, strongest man in the whole wide world. If tolerable meant finding the exact right place to land

If it meant setting out for adventure with a soulmate at her side.

Hank dropped a kiss on the top of her head. "You're my favorite kind of trouble." Then he whispered something in her ear that made her cheeks go red.

Tolerable, indeed.

PREVIEW OF HEAT

Keep reading for a preview of the fourth book in The Firefighters of Darling Bay series, Heat.

HEAT - CHAPTER 1

"It's a right turn, here." Bonnie pointed out the ambulance window. "At the post office."

Caswell Lloyd ignored her, blowing past the turn. The siren blared, and two children in a crosswalk waved.

"Caz?" Bonnie waved back at the kids and then blew out a breath, thumping backward into her seat. "Fine. If you think you know where you're going better than I do, even though you've worked this zone, for what, like five minutes?"

He didn't even have the grace to look her direction as he turned right at the bookstore.

Bonnie bit the inside of her mouth to keep from saying another word. They'd been on three calls so far that day, and he'd been like this on all of them, taciturn, practically non-verbal, and now he wasn't even driving in the right direction. He was going to have to double back half a block. Precious seconds would be lost, seconds that might mean the difference between life and death...

Well. Since they were responding to a medical alarm at

Ava Simon's house, the chances were pretty good it wasn't that big a deal. When Ava's grandkids had given her the medical pendant a year before, she'd spent the first two months pushing it just "to see how fast you could get here."

Bonnie hated change in her ambulance. Just when she'd finally gotten used to her partner, she'd gotten stuck with someone new. Johnny Kling, her last partner, had taken her six months to train, and then he'd been promoted to firefighter and transferred to Engine Three, moving Caz up the list to Station One. Of course, Johnny took the transfer. They all went somewhere—anywhere—to get off the ambo.

The problem lay in the fact that a lot of the guys, although they were all paramedics, didn't actually *want* to be on the ambulance. Ever. They wanted to do their paramedic time and mark it off their checklists. They wanted to hurry up and promote. Then they could do what they really wanted to do which was roll code three to the calls in their nice, clean engines, assess the patient, save a life with some simple CPR if they could, and then hand that patient over to Bonnie and whoever she was paired with for the difficult and stressful transport to the hospital—drives during which the recently-saved patient might code and have to be restarted all over again, while the vehicle flew fifty miles-per-hour around curves. It didn't help that the medics were the ones who spent hours waiting for busy hospital staff to take over care of patients, not the firefighters. The medics (not the firefighters) were the ones who ended up covered in vomit or worse. Who cleaned out the ambulance after a particularly gross call? Bonnie and her partner did.

The thing was, Bonnie freaking loved it. Maybe few others did, but she knew she belonged on the ambulance. She'd taken and passed all the classes, her log books were signed off. She could promote to firefighter during any testing phase. But she didn't want to. Riding in the back of the ambulance, pushing the morphine and then holding the hand of a person who was more scared than they'd ever been in their whole lives? Nothing was better than being the person who got to look a terrified patient in the eye and reassure them that yes, she was going to be just fine.

Even if it was—an awful lot of the time—a lie.

It was a lie Bonnie Maddern was honored to tell, a lie she believed every time she told it. Because if she didn't believe her patient was going to make it, who would?

Caz had figured out his mistake and made the correct turn.

"There," Bonnie said, gesturing to the old house. It was covered in peeling olive paint, and upstairs, a broken window was held together with blue painter's tape. A yellowed curtain hung crookedly at one window, and a rusted bicycle missing one wheel was upside down in what might have been a garden at one time.

Caz still hadn't said a word to her.

Fantastic.

Bonnie hadn't spent much time with Caz since he'd joined the department two years before. He'd been consistently assigned to a different house, and they'd only crossed on overtime shifts, never partnered. He'd always seemed a bit too cocksure, too confident, with that wide cowboy walk of his that took up too much of the hallway now that he was at Station One. It was too bad he was so good-looking, the rancher version of Matthew McConaughey. Caz's intensely light blue eyes made it startling to run into him in the dayroom. It made him a little less easy to ignore.

But heck. There was no rule they *had* to talk on the

ambulance, aside from what was necessary to the job. They didn't have to be friends. It was only ten days a month, she told herself. She could handle anything ten days a month, even a guy like Caz. Walking up the driveway in silence with him, Bonnie realized she was actually missing Jimmy's persistent throat-clearing.

Bonnie knocked on the door.

No answer.

Caz reached around her and knocked louder. Yeah, he probably thought he could even do that better than she could.

From inside, they heard a woman yell, "It's open!"

Inside, the house appeared somewhat clean. That was just about all it had going for it. The decades-old wallpaper —green and yellow stripes—was in as good repair as the peeling paint outside. The thin orange carpet at their feet must have been installed in the sixties or seventies. It smelled, as always, of garlic and lentils and something sweet, maybe a tropical air freshener.

In a tattered recliner sat Ava, an elderly woman who looked as if she'd been in place for as many years as the carpet. "Hello, hello!" Her curly white hair was tucked neatly behind her ears, and she wore three pairs of glasses— one on top of her head, one on her face, and one hung around her neck by a long blue plastic cord.

"Hiya," said Caz easily. Oh, so he *could* talk.

Bonnie came forward with her bag. "What's going on today, Mrs. Simon?" There was no television in the sparely furnished room, just a couch and a small red table with two matching wooden chairs. She wasn't holding a book, nor was there anything in her lap. Had she just been sitting there? For how long?

Caz reached forward, "Caswell Lloyd, ma'am. Pleasure to meet you. I'm new on the ambulance."

He was trying to charm her? He knew how?

"Ava Simon," the woman said. "So glad you've come. I wish I could offer you a cup of coffee, but I'm fresh out."

"Not to worry. I had my required pot before I left the station." He crouched in front of her, smiling. "What can we do for you today? How are you feeling?"

At least the man was a little less scary-looking when he smiled. He went from resembling the Matthew McConaughey of *True Detective* to the one in *Magic Mike*.

The woman's face brightened. "Oh, my. I'm just fine, thank you for asking, you big hunk of good-looking, you."

Bonnie stepped forward. "All righty. Let's get a read on your blood pressure. Did you take your medicine today?"

Ava frowned at her and pushed away the BP cuff. Sitting forward, she peered around Bonnie and smiled at Caz. "Caswell Lloyd, you said? Any relation to Harrison Lloyd?"

"My grandfather, ma'am."

"Oh," said Ava with a giggle. "I had such a crush on him years ago, when we attended the same church. Such a fine man he was. And handsome! Just like you. You got your blue eyes from him, eh?"

"Thank you kindly, ma'am. Now. What's the problem today?"

Ava batted her lashes at Caz. "It's my toilet, honey. Something's just not right."

"Your toilet?" sputtered Bonnie. "That's why you pushed your alarm? Okay, that's just not—"

Caz cut her off. "I'm sure Bonnie won't mind giving that a quick look while I look at something a little prettier. Mind if I take your pulse?"

Bonnie stomped down the hall. The guy had *nerve.*

Plumbing was the worst. There was a reason she didn't work the truck with its water removal tools. She hated the way water glugged through a clogged pipe and she literally had to call a plumber to get the hair out of her own bath drain—the look of a sodden clump of gunk being pulled out was enough to make her gag.

Working on someone else's toilet *really* wasn't what she'd gone into the fire profession to do.

But it was better than watching Caz Lloyd flirt with Ava Simon. How was she going to work a whole *year* with him?

Five minutes later, after quite a bit of plunging accompanied by increasingly creative under-her-breath cursing, the toilet was almost clear. She could hear Caz and Ava laughing.

Oh, good. They were having a fine time while she used brute force and listened to pipes gurgle angrily.

"I'm doing fine! Thanks for asking!" Bonnie blew her short blond hair out of her eyes. She gave one final shove of the plunger, but she did such a fine job of it that she couldn't pull it back out again. She put one foot against the toilet and pulled harder. "Dang it, do *not* tick me off, you old porcelain bucket, you." One more pull.

With a small scream, Bonnie toppled backward as the toilet came off its seal, pulling away from the wall. There was a crash as the porcelain bowl and tank smashed into a thousand pieces, followed by a flood of dirty water that covered her from the waist down. The brown water was quickly followed by a frigid high-pressure spray of clean water, which jetted out of the pipe in the wall, hitting her in the face.

From the living room she heard Caz roar, "What's going on in there?"

"Don't worry!" she yelled back. "I've got this!" Then she drummed her legs against the floor in a quick wordless fit, took a moment set her lips into a determined and very firmly closed line. Then she lunged at the pipe.

CHAPTER 2

I t was Caz's turn to cook, his first night at Station One. Seeing as he'd already gotten crap from two of the guys for browning the meat too well on the industrial stove's huge burners, it wasn't going great so far. Not that he cared that much. He wasn't here to make friends, after all.

Tox Ellis, the engine's captain, leaned over his shoulder. "That's too many onions. Coin is gonna throw a fit."

Caz didn't respond. It was usually the best course of action, he'd found.

"You gonna take some out or what?"

Did the guy actually think he was going to redo dinner because of someone's preference? "No."

"Coin *really* hates onions."

"Then I guess he can make his own damn dinner."

Tox grunted. "You came from Los Robles FD, right?"

Caz nodded. Was he going to have to talk right up until the food was on the table? Was that a requirement here? The way Bonnie Maddern chattered on the ambulance, it might well be.

"You worked with John Martini?"

He nodded again. Hopefully, the guy would get the hint. He didn't want to be out and out rude—next to the battalion chief, it was clear that Tox ruled the roost around this station. It wouldn't do to get on his bad side. But when Caz cooked, he liked doing it in silence.

Heck, he liked doing just about everything in silence. He thought of Bonnie again. Never quiet, except after that last run when she'd been covered in toilet water.

Tox popped a piece of red pepper in his mouth.

Caz *hated* it when people messed with his cooking. "Do you mind?"

The man's thick eyebrows rose? "Not really. I like peppers. You got plenty. So, you and Martini get along?"

Martini had been a blowhard engineer with britches that were about a mile too big for his five-foot-nothing frame. It was better not to answer. "Is anyone going to mind garlic?"

"Nah. What about Horton, is he still a battalion chief there?"

"Yeah."

"Good guy, huh?"

Horton was one of the most boring people he'd ever met in his life. But he wasn't bad. "I guess."

"You're a tough nut, huh?"

"Look, I just want to cook these carnitas and get it over with. That okay with you?"

"What's your problem?" Tox's voice didn't seem to carry the normal venom that went with those words. He seemed honestly curious. And no way was Caz going to confide in him.

"Hand me the cayenne?"

Tox sighed and gave over the Costco-sized container. "Whatever. You don't have to have friends here, man, but a forty-eight hour shift is long. It goes easier if you play well with others."

"I hear you."

"There anything else you want to say?"

Caz stopped and looked directly at the man. "I have no idea what you want from me."

"Man," said Tox, clearly at the end of his friendly tolerance. He'd lasted longer than most. "How about chill the freak out?" He stalked out of the kitchen.

Caz focused on the blade of his knife. Pineapple, instead of making the meat sweet, tenderized it. And it was satisfying to chop. He thunked off the top and the bottom, then whacked at the sides of it.

"What's that?" His next kitchen intruder was the tall engineer named Hank Coffee. He seemed nice enough, more mellow than Tox, but he was part of the house's noise and bluster, too.

"A pineapple," said Caz simply.

"I'm allergic."

"Okay." He didn't stop chopping.

"Are you really going to put that in dinner?"

"Yes."

"Even though I told you I'm allergic?"

Caz's knife slowed and he looked up. "I figured Tox told you to say that. Are you really?"

Hank blinked. "No."

"Okay, then."

Hank leaned against the counter easily, as if he had nowhere better to be. "So tell me about yourself."

Caz hated open-ended questions that weren't really even questions at all. "Nothing much to tell."

"You married?"

He also hated yes or no questions. "Nope."

"Kids?"

"Nope." Caz finished chopping the pineapple and dumped it into the pork shoulder on the stove.

"You live nearby?"

"Nope."

"Dude. You make it hard to talk to you, anyone ever tell you that?"

"Heard it said."

Hank didn't give up, though. "Okay, then, where do you live? Exactly?"

Maybe if Caz answered a couple of questions, he'd go away. "About fifteen miles outside town, due east out 119."

"There's nothing out there."

Well, on one hand that was true, there was a whole lot of nothing near Caz's ranch. But that was the best part of it. Nothing and no one. "We raise horses. My dad does." *Did.*

"Well, that's something." Hank looked cheered. "You're a cowboy. That explains the hat in your truck."

"What were you doing looking in my truck?"

"I was snooping," said Hank cheerfully. "I do that. Who takes care of your horses while you're at work?"

"My foreman."

"Fancy! You got a foreman! Is it a dude ranch? Can I come out and ride?"

"No."

"Why not?" Just like Tox, Hank seemed curiously friendly.

And Caz was tired of avoiding the question. "I don't like people very much."

"Firefighters? Citizens? Men? Women? *All* people?"

Caz slid the pre-chopped onions into the pot and turned the heat to high. "Pretty much all of 'em."

"Yeah, see, I don't believe that."

"You should."

"Nah," said Hank. "I talked to your field training officer, Bert."

Caz's FTO at Los Robles FD had been a man who never, ever, *ever* shut up. "Huh."

"Yeah. And he said that when it comes to patient care, you're right up there with the best he's seen."

Caz just added more cayenne. Maybe he could burn his new coworkers' chit-chat buds right off.

"And what I think is that goes directly against what I've seen from you in this house. You don't talk, you don't smile, you don't laugh. But Bert says you make people feel safe. And that's not a thing that someone who doesn't like people does." Hank paused as if he thought Caz might say something. When he didn't speak, Hank went on, "So that makes me feel better, at least, because you're kind of acting like a tool around here. I'm willing to put that down to nerves."

That's not what it was. Not at all. Caz added a healthy dose of cumin to the pot.

"Do you even want to be here?" Hank's voice was tighter now.

"I do." That was the simplest answer to a complex question.

"Did you like your last department?"

"Not really."

"Why did you leave?"

Caz sighed. "I didn't get along with staff."

"Surprise, surprise. Do you like it here better, so far?"

"No." Especially not if he was going to have to put up with Bonnie Maddern as a partner for the next year. How was he supposed to ignore someone as pretty and *pushy* as she was? But what could he do? It seemed like the woman could talk the hind leg off a donkey, and probably would if given half a chance. It didn't help that she was so dang pretty sometimes he forgot to mind that she was talking. Her short blond bob was always a little uneven, as if she'd woken up and just run her fingers through it to smooth it—yeah, her hair bothered Caz, mostly because he found his fingers itching to see if it felt as soft as it looked.

He hadn't taken the Darling Bay job in order to meet a woman, though.

Paying for his father's care was why Caz had applied for and accepted the higher-paying job, even as far away from his cabin as it was.

Caz knew himself. He could put up with just about anything. They could pair him up with Tox (talk about someone who *never* shut up) or make him clean the bathrooms every day. He was the FNG, after all, the freaking new guy. Caz just wanted to come to work, do his job, collect his paycheck, and go home. That surely couldn't be too much to ask.

Hank laughed. "So you seriously don't like being here? Jeez. Why stay then?"

"Because I think it's a good department. I think I can learn to like it. Or at least tolerate it."

"You always this dang honest?"

"Yes."

"Why not just stay on your ranch and raise horses?"

"Not enough money in it." That was the sad truth. For Dad's full-time care, Caz needed a full-time job. That was the bitter catch-22.

Hank's eyes were bright. He was enjoying this give and take, even if Caz wasn't. "Do you like *horses*, at least?"

"Not really." Caz was a woodworker, not a horse man. But where did these guys get the idea that you got to like what you did for a living?

"You are a cranky sum-gun, ain'tcha?"

"I've heard that on occasion, too."

Hank rapped his empty plastic cup against the counter firmly. "Well. I'll let you alone, then."

Finally.

"But I gotta say one thing. There're good men in this department. Good women, too, just outnumbered. You got one riding in your ambulance with you. There's no reason you can't make friends here. But you gotta want to."

Caz knew that. He turned up the heat again and poked the meat with a wooden spoon.

He heard the kitchen door swing shut behind Hank. Alone again.

Good.

CHAPTER 3

The nice thing about the women's bathroom at Station One, the thing that the men's didn't have, was a glazed window in the shower. It was always closed for safety, of course. You wouldn't want a random drunk citizen hauling himself in and roaming the station halls in the middle of the night. But when Bonnie was in the shower, there was no harm in her sliding the window open. Like a dog propping a chin on a car windowsill, Bonnie rested her chin on the tiled ledge, resting her eyes on the long swathe of green grass behind the station. It was marred a little by the big concrete driveway that ran through the apparatus bay, but that was a necessary evil. On the other side of the drive was a stand of eucalyptus trees that went right down to the creek that was still rushing with the March rains. Around dinner time, the frogs who lived on its banks started their deafening chorus. The wild California poppies that dotted their edges of the station lawn had shut for the night even though twilight hadn't fully settled.

It was her favorite time of night. And this was her

favorite thing to do—to stand in the hot shower, watching the quiet riverbank. At any moment, the tones could go off in the station, and four minutes later—still damp under her hastily-thrown-on uniform—she might be on the road, bouncing up and down in the tech seat, racing for whatever disaster (or stubbed toe) had prompted one of the Darling Bay citizens to dial 911. But the tones stayed blessedly quiet. The frogs chirruped. A soft breeze sighed in the tall eucalyptus, and Bonnie, her body and hair newly sewage-free, closed her eyes in happiness.

This was, truly, the life. She couldn't be any luckier. She heard her mother's voice in her head, "Everything is good when you look at it from the right direction." Heck, even getting doused by disgusting toilet water meant that she got to hang out in the shower at a time when she wasn't keeping any of the other women in the station from taking theirs. All the other women in the station, of course, were dispatchers, since Bonnie was the only female firefighter on A shift. The dispatchers tended to take their showers as soon as they woke up in the morning, and since their hours were more tightly scheduled, Bonnie tried to stay out of their way as much as possible.

The water beating against her back was gloriously hot. She redirected it so that it hit more of her as she turned so she could rest her cheek against the window's ledge. The cool air of the spring night blew on the crown of her wet hair. She kept her eyes closed and sighed in pleasure.

The breeze got stronger. Huh. Warmer, too. She waited for the evening air to shift, but instead, she smelled mint.

Mint gum. Spearmint, to be exact. Like someone was standing outside blowing on her head.

She opened her eyes and jerked her head upright, but

she didn't quite avoid the light slap aimed at her cheek. Tox, standing outside in the flower border, roared with laughter. She slammed the window shut and yelled through it, "You jacknut! I could have died! I could have slipped and *died* and then you'd be back on the ambulance and you'd be *so sorry!*"

Bonnie heard more male laughter join Tox's. She sighed. At least there was no way he could have peeked in downward. The worst he'd seen was the top of her wet head. Good thing, too. If he'd seen more, Bonnie would have cheerfully called his girlfriend Grace from the day room so everyone could listen, and she would have taken great pleasure in telling Grace what her big dumb captain boyfriend had done. Bonnie pulled down her towel and dried herself.

Idiot boys. It was like living with eight big brothers.

She pulled on her uniform roughly, not caring the backs of her knees and spine weren't totally dry. Speed was important while getting dressed at the station. She'd been tempting fate wasting time in the shower anyway.

The six o'clock tone buzzed overhead, and over the intercom, Tox yelled, "Dinner! Dinner time."

Bonnie checked with dispatch before going down to the kitchen. Only Lexie was working, Sue must have already been in the dorm on her sleep shift. "You eating with us tonight?"

Lexie looked over her computer screen, her red curls crazily piled on her head, her smile bright. "Nope! I'm good!"

"Dang, you're cheerful. What's up with you?" Bonnie tapped the tiny firefighter wind chime that dangled next to Lexie's terminal, making it tinkle softly.

"Um…"

From the floor behind Lexie's terminal, Coin Keefe said, "Hiya." He was lying on the floor on his back, next to Lexie's chair.

"Holy—" What had she interrupted? "Get a room, you two!"

"It's not what it looks like," said Coin.

Bonnie looked at Lexie for an answer, but she was giggling too hard to answer.

Slowly, Coin sat up. "You know I got that neck pain." He pointed to the pillow he'd been lying on. It was covered with tiny plastic spikes.

"Oh, no," said Bonnie, backing up, her hands in front of her. "Seriously. If that's some kind of kink, I so don't need to know. At *all*. Private lives should be kept that way…"

Lexie laughed harder and then finally choked out, "It's an acupressure pillow. Grace gave it to me when my neck was bothering me, and it's been helping Coin. He just didn't want y'all down the hall to know."

Bonnie raised an eyebrow. "So that's the only reason he's hiding out of sight behind your work station?"

Blushing, Lexie nodded. Coin, never the most outgoing of Bonnie's shift mates, said, "And that's my cute. Dang. I mean my cue…" He hurriedly dropped a kiss on Lexie head and raced out of dispatch.

Lexie, finally bringing herself under control, said, "He's ridiculous. I have no idea why I put up with him."

Bonnie sank into a chair. "You're crazy about him."

Lexie ducked her head. "Anyway. What's up? Why aren't you eating?"

"I'm going to. Wanted to see if you wanted anything."

"Nah." Lexie waved a hand at a plate of rice and beans on her terminal. "I've been picking at this for hours. I'm fine."

"Cold food isn't the same as fresh, warm stuff."

"Dispatchers are used to cold food." 911 rang. Lexie reached for the button and said, "Speaking of which..." While she questioned the caller over her headset, she dispatched Engine Three and Medic Five using her foot pedal.

"No, ma'am, don't slap him on the back. That could push the marble farther into his windpipe. Just keep him still." She gave a kind laugh. "I know, it's hard with a three-year-old to keep him from climbing around. I know you're doing a great job. I'll just keep you on the line till the first unit pulls up, okay? You let me know when you hear the siren."

Without asking, Bonnie picked up Lexie's plate, added a sprinkle more of cheese on top, and zapped it in the microwave. By the time the engine was on scene and Lexie had hung up, her food was warm again.

"You didn't need to do that."

"I know," said Bonnie. "But you're just so *stuck* in this cage."

"Hey, I like my cage. It fits me."

Bonnie rubbed the edge of the round table. It was slightly sticky, and that, unlike Lexie's food temperature, was none of her business. She had to spend enough time cleaning the kitchen and day room with the rest of the guys —she didn't need to clean in here, too. "Your cage doesn't get to roll lights-and-sirens to anything."

"My cage doesn't need to be mopped down for blood."

Bonnie pointed at the stickiness on the table. "For germs, though."

"Dang it," said Lexie. "I *told* Sue she had to clean up after using her dang pressure cooker, but she never listens."

The firehouse was a family. And it was a nice thing, of

course. The camaraderie that automatically came with the job was something Bonnie loved. What most people didn't know, though, was how dysfunctionally family-like fire-houses could be. It wasn't funny or cute when one captain refused to *ever* rinse a plate before sticking it in the rather mediocre dishwasher. When PeeWee left the house's groceries on the counter for six hours because he didn't "feel" like putting them in the fridge, and three of them got sick on the pork as a result, they weren't grateful PeeWee was a fire brother. No, just like any other brother who screwed up, the firefighters had hated his guts for a good week. He'd had to clean the station bathrooms for a month in penance, and that was no small punishment.

Lexie got out a wet wipe to scrub at the spot.

"Later," said Bonnie. "Eat your food, lady. Before you fall over from hunger."

Lexie patted her not-very-thin waistline. With her bright red hair and lips and her blue uniform, she looked a little like a pinup girl stuck in the wrong clothes. "Do I look like I'm suffering? If Coin and his daughter don't quit making me those caramel turtle cookies, I'm going to need to get a new pair of uniform pants, stat."

"Yeah, I think Coin likes you just fine the way you are."

Lexie grinned and reached for her plate. "Yeah, I guess. He likes a girl with handles. And hey, I like the way he handles me. Oh, how did that last call go? Why did you have to return for cleanup if you didn't even transport the patient?"

Bonnie groaned. "It's what's-his-name's fault."

"The new guy? Caz..." Lexie scrabbled for her Telestaff roster. "Caswell Lloyd, that's it. I've only met him once. He's your new partner, right?"

Sighing, Bonnie said, "Yeah. Because he was too busy flirting with old Mrs. Simon, I had to deal with why she pushed her medical alert."

"Which was..."

"Her toilet."

"Oh, no."

"Oh, yes."

"She's been getting pretty bad lately. I worked overtime the other day on C shift and I took a call from the alarm company. She pushed the button because she couldn't get her beer open."

"You're *kidding*."

"I sent one of the rounds guys instead of a full engine, but apparently she yelled at him after he dropped the beer —it was her only bottle— and he came back looking pretty pale. I felt kind of bad for him. So you had to, what? Plunge a backup?" Lexie snorted.

"I wish. That's how it started, but it turned out that while they were out in the living room yukking it up, I might have been a little too...emphatic in my plunging."

"Mmm?" Lexie folded in her lips and her eyes danced.

"I yanked the whole thing off its seal because of the slant of her old crooked floor, and the whole thing tipped over. It crashed."

"As in broke?" Lexie covered her mouth.

"As in shattered. I was covered in—"

Lexie held up a hand. "I'm eating."

"You can eat through anything! I've seen you drink a milkshake while listening to a guy vomit in your ear."

"That's different. That's far away." Lexie wrinkled her nose in Bonnie's direction. "You, you're closer. You were covered in...poop. And then you put *cheese* on my *plate*."

"I took a shower! A long one! New clothes!"

"Hmmm." Lexie appeared to be considering whether or not to let her stay. "I suppose…"

Bonnie stood. "Fine, I have to eat dinner anyway."

"Wait, wait. What did you do?"

"What could I do? That's why we were out of service so long. I had to clean and disinfect her whole bathroom and remove the rubble. Then we went to the hardware store, where I bought her a new toilet."

"Your own money?"

"Can you even imagine what Susie Costello would do if I turned it in for reimbursement? She'd deny it so fast she'd get a nosebleed."

Lexie laughed.

Bonnie glared. "You're not being very helpful for someone who says she's in the helping business."

"You put it in? Yourself?"

Straightening her shoulders, Bonnie nodded. "Turns out I'm good with plumbing. Even though I *hate* it. I even added one of those fancy new seat-warmer bidets."

"Holy crap. Pun intended."

Bonnie couldn't help smiling. Mrs. Simon had really liked the idea of it, giving her a smile that had up till that point been reserved for Caz. And pleasing her had been the goal. If it kept Mrs. Simon from filing a complaint, then Bonnie didn't mind the couple hundred bucks she'd dropped to do it.

No, what she minded was the way Caz Lloyd had handled himself on the call. "So you're saying you don't know anything about the new guy?"

Lexie shook her head. "Just that he lateraled in from a department up north. Los Robles, maybe? I can't remember. People say he's pretty quiet."

Not with Mrs. Simon, he hadn't been. He'd been all charm, as if the old woman had tapped his side for maple syrup. But in the rig on the way to the hardware store, he'd just stared straight ahead as he drove. His only change of facial expression had been when he'd rolled down his window and the airflow wafted her stench over him. "Noxious," he'd muttered.

Bonnie had been too irritated to say anything at all.

"Caz helped you install the toilet, though, didn't he?" Lexie's eyes sparkled.

"You're loving this, aren't you?"

The dispatcher nodded. "Best story I've heard all day."

"No, he did *not*. And I hate him for it." Any other of her coworkers would have been in the bathroom with her, manhandling the pipes and telling her she was doing it wrong but helping anyway. "What he did was sit in Mrs. Simon's kitchen while she made him—and I'm not making this up—fresh peanut butter cookies. Meanwhile, I installed a new toilet, hooked up an electric bidet, and sanitized a room that was disgusting even before I dumped dirty toilet water all over it."

"Did you get a cookie?"

Bonnie's face burned. "I asked for one."

"They denied you?"

"He said I should clean up first or risk giving myself a disease."

"Did he bring one back for you?"

"You know he didn't."

Lexie said, "All right. He's on my to-be-woken-at-one-a.m. list."

Bonnie nodded in satisfaction. "That's all I'm asking. Hey! No, wait. I'm his partner! If you wake him, you wake me."

"Just enjoy his pain, my friend." Lexie gave her patented grin and Bonnie was grateful all over again to have the job she did. There was nothing better than working with friends.

She'd just *make* Caz become one. Whether he liked it or not.

KEEP READING!

Keep reading by grabbing *Heat* now! Just go to RachaelHerronBooks.com to get your copy!

(Psst - there are special discounts over there, too!)

ABOUT RACHAEL

Rachael Herron is the internationally bestselling author of more than twenty books, including thriller (under R.H. Herron), mainstream fiction, romance, memoir, and nonfiction about writing. She received her MFA in writing from Mills College, Oakland, and she teaches writing extension workshops at both UC Berkeley and Stanford. She's a New Zealand citizen as well as an American.

She'd *love* to hear from you! Sign up for her mailing list at RachaelHerron.com/Subscribe, then drop her a line and she'll write you back! (Seriously. She loves to hear from readers.) Plus you'll get a free short love story that will melt your heart, instantly! Or find her on social media!

instagram.com/rachaelherron

patreon.com/rachael

facebook.com/Rachael.Herron.Author

bookbub.com/authors/rachael-herron

youtube.com/@RachaelHerronWrites